# The Collected Supernatural and Weird Fiction of Thomas Graham Jackson
# —Six Ghost Stories—

# The Collected Supernatural and Weird Fiction of Thomas Graham Jackson —Six Ghost Stories—

Two Novelettes and
Four Shorter Tales
to Chill the Blood

Thomas Graham Jackson

LEONAUR

*The Collected*
*Supernatural and Weird*
*Fiction of*
*Thomas Graham Jackson*
*—Six Ghost Stories—*
*Two Novelettes and Four Shorter Tales*
*to Chill the Blood*
by Thomas Graham Jackson

First published under the title
*Six Ghost Stories*

Leonaur is an imprint
of Oakpast Ltd

ISBN: 978-1-84677-850-6 (hardcover)
ISBN: 978-1-84677-849-0 (softcover)

http://www.leonaur.com

# Contents

# The Lady of Rosemount

'And so, Charlton, you're going to spend part of the Long at Rosemount Abbey. I envy you. It's an awfully jolly old place, and you'll have a really good time.'

'Yes,' said Charlton, 'I am looking forward to it immensely. I have never seen it; you know it has only lately come to my uncle and they only moved into it last Christmas, I forgot that you knew it and had been there.'

'Oh! I don't know it very well,' said Edwards: 'I spent a few days there a year or two ago with the last owner. It will suit you down to the ground, for you are mad about old abbeys and ruins, and you'll find enough there to satisfy the whole Society of Antiquaries as well as yourself. When do you go?'

'Very soon. I must be at home for a week or so after we go down, and then I think my uncle will expect me at Rosemount. What are you going to do?'

'Well! I hardly know. Nothing very exciting. Perhaps take a short run abroad a little later. But I shall have to read part of the Long, for I am in for Greats next term. By the way, it is just possible I may be somewhere in your direction, for I have friends near Rosemount who want me to spend part of the vac. down there.'

'All right,' said Charlton, 'don't forget to come over and see me. I hope I may still be there. Meanwhile, *au revoir*, old man, and good luck to you.'

Charlton remained some time at his window looking on the quad of his college. Term at Oxford was just over and the men were rapidly going down. Hansoms were waiting at the gate, scouts and messengers were clattering down the staircases with portmanteaux and other paraphernalia proper to youth, and piling them on the cabs, friends were shaking hands, and bidding goodbye. In a few hours the college would be empty, and solitude would descend upon it for four months, broken only by occasional visitors, native or transatlantic. The flight of the men would be followed by that of the Dons to all parts of Europe or beyond, the hive would be deserted, and the porter would reign supreme over a vast solitude, monarch of all he surveyed.

Charlton was not due to go down till the next morning. He dined in the junior common-room with three or four other men, the sole survivors of the crowd, and then retired to his rooms to finish his packing. That done, he sat on the window-seat looking into the quad. It was a brilliant night; the moonshine slept on the grass, and silvered the grey walls and mullioned windows opposite, while the chapel and hall were plunged in impenetrable shadow. Everything was as still as death; no sound from the outer world penetrated the enclosure, and for the busy hive of men within, there was now the silence of a desert. There is perhaps no place where silence and solitude can be more sensibly felt than the interior of an Oxford college in vacation time, and there was something in the scene that appealed to the temperament of the young man who regarded it.

Henry Charlton was an only child. His father had died when he was a lad, and his mother, broken down by grief, had foresworn society and lived a very retired life in the country. At Winchester and Oxford he naturally mixed with others and made acquaintances, but his home life was somewhat sombre and his society restricted. He grew up a self-contained, reserved lad, with a few friendships, though those he formed were sincere and his attachments were strong. His temperament—poetical, and tinged with melancholy—naturally inclined to romance, and from his early youth he delighted in antiquarian pursuits, heraldic lore, and legend.

At school and college he revelled in the ancient architecture by which he was surrounded. His tastes even carried him further, into the region of physical research, and the dubious revelations of spiritualism; though a certain wholesome vein of scepticism saved him from plunging deeply into those mazes, whether of truth or imposture. As he sat at his window, the familiar scene put on an air of romance. The silence sank into his soul; the windows where a friendly light was wont to shine through red curtains, inviting a visit, were now blind and dark; mystery enveloped the well-known walls; they seemed a place for the dead, no longer a habitation for living men, of whom he might be the last survivor. At last, rising from his seat, and half-laughing at his own romantic fancies, Henry Charlton went to bed.

A few weeks later he descended from the train at the little country station of Brickhill, in Northamptonshire, and while the porter was collecting his traps on a hand-barrow, he looked out for the carriage that was to meet him. 'Hallo! Harry, here you are,' said a voice behind him, and turning round he was warmly greeted by his cousin, Charley Wilmot. A car was waiting, into which he and his belongings were packed, and in five minutes they were off, bowling along one of the wide Northamptonshire roads, with a generous expanse of green-sward on each side between the hedges, and the hedgerow timber.

The country was new to Henry Charlton, and he looked about him with interest. The estate of Rosemount had lately come unexpectedly by the death of a distant relation of his uncle, Sir Thomas Wilmot, and the family had hardly had time yet to settle down in their new home. His cousin Charley was full of the novelty of the situation, and the charms of the Abbey.

'I can tell you, it's a rattling old place,' said he, 'full of odd holes and corners, and there are the ruins of the church with all sorts of old things to be seen; but you'll have lots of time to look about and see it all, and here we are, and there's my dad waiting to welcome you at the hall-door.'

They had turned in at a lodge-gate, and passed up an avenue at the end of which Henry could see a hoary pile of stone gables, mullioned windows, massive chimneys, and a wide-arched portal, hospitably open, where Sir Thomas stood to welcome his nephew.

Some years had passed since Henry had seen his relatives, and he was glad to be with them again. A houseful of lively cousins, rather younger than himself, had in former days afforded a welcome change from his own melancholy home, and he looked forward with pleasure to renewing the intimacy. His young cousin Charley was just at the end of his time at Eton, and was to go to university in October. The girls, Kate and Cissy, had shot up since he used to play with them in the nursery, and were now too old to be kissed. His uncle and aunt were as kind as ever, and after he had answered their inquiries about his mother, and given an account of his uneventful journey down, the whole party adjourned to the garden where tea awaited them under the trees, and then Henry for the first time saw something of the Abbey of Rosemount.

This ancient foundation of *Sanctus Egidius in Monte Rosarum* had been a Benedictine house, dating from the twelfth century, which at the Dissolution was granted to a royal favourite, who partly dismantled and partly converted it into a residence for himself. His descendants in the time of James I had pulled down a great part of the conventual buildings and substituted for the inconvenient cells of the monks a more comfortable structure in the style of that day. Many fragments of the Abbey, however, were incorporated into the later house. The refectory of the monks was kept, and formed the great hall of the mansion with its vaulted roof and traceried windows, in which there even remained some of the old storied glass.

The Abbot's kitchen still furnished Sir Thomas's hospitable board, and among the offices and elsewhere were embedded parts of the domestic buildings. North of the refectory, according to the usual Benedictine plan, had been the cloister and beyond that the church, which lay at a slightly lower level, the lie of the ground inclining that way from the summit of the Mount of Roses on which the habitable part of the convent had been built. Of the cloister enough remained, though much broken and dilapidated, to show what it had been, but the greater part of the church was destroyed for the sake of its materials when the Jacobean house was built. A considerable part of the nave, however, was still standing, part of it even with its vaulted roof intact, and of the rest, enough of the lower part of the walls was left to show that the church had been of a fair size, though not on the scale of the larger establishments.

Henry Charlton, with the greedy eye of the born antiquary, took in the general scheme of the Abbey with his tea and buttered toast under the shade of the elms that bounded the lawn on the side of the house. But he had to control his impatience to visit the ruins, for after tea his cousins insisted on a game of tennis, which lasted till it was time to dress for dinner, and after dinner it was too late and too dark foe exploration.

They dined in the great hall, once the monk's refectory, but not too large for modem comfort, the Abbey having been one of the smaller houses of the Order, and the number of the brotherhood limited. Henry was enchanted and could not restrain the expression of his enthusiasm.

'Ah!' said his aunt, 'I remember your mother told me you were crazy about architecture and antiquities. Well, you'll have your fill of them here. For my part, I often sigh for a little more modern convenience.'

'But my dear aunt,' said Henry, 'there is so much to make up for a little inconveniences in living in this lovely old place that they might be forgotten.'

'Why, what do you know about housekeeping?' said his aunt, 'I should like you to hear Mrs Baldwin, the housekeeper, on the subject. How she toils up one staircase only to have to go down another. The house, she says, is made up of stairs that are not wanted, and crooked passages that might not have been straight, and it took the maids a fortnight to learn their way to the food-store.'

'It's no use,' said Charley, 'you'll never convince him. He would like to have those old monks back again, and be one of them himself with a greasy cowl on his head and sandals on his naked feet, and nothing to eat but herbs washed down with water.'

'No, no!' said Henry laughing, 'I don't want them back, for I like my present company too well. But I confess I like to call up in imagination the men who built and lived in these old walls, I believe I shall dream of them tonight.'

'Well, Henry,' said his uncle, 'you may dream of them as much as you please, so long as you don't bring them back to us to turn us out. And you shall have every opportunity, for you are to sleep in a bit of the old convent that the abbey builders of the modern house spared; and who knows but that ghost of its former occupant may not take you at your word and come back to revisit his old quarters.'

Henry laughed as they rose from table, and said he trusted his visitor would not treat him as an intruder.

The long summer day had enabled them to finish dinner by daylight, and there was still light enough for the old painted glass to be seen. It was very fragmentary, and not one of the pictures was perfect. In one of the lights they could make out part of a female figure richly dressed; she had been holding something that was broken away, and beside her was the lower half of an unmistakable demon, with hairy legs and cloven hoof. The legend below ran thus, the last word being imperfect:

QVALITER DIABOLVS TENTAVIT COMITISSAM ALI . . .

The next light was still more imperfect, but there was part of the same female figure in violent action, with the fragment of a legend:

HIC COMITISSA TENTATA A DI . . .

Other parts evidently of the same story remained in the next window, but they were too fragmentary to be understood. In one light was a piece of a monk's figure and part of a legend:

HIC FRATER PAVLVS DAT COMI . . .

The last of all was tolerably perfect. It represented a female robed in black, and holding in her hand a little model of a church. She was on her knees prostrate before the Pope, who was seated and extended his hand in the act of benediction. The legend below said:

*HIC COMITISSA A PAPA ABSOLVTA EST.*

Henry was much interested and wanted to know the story of the sinful Countess; but none of the party could tell him, and indeed, none of them had till then paid much attention to the glass. Sir Thomas had once made a slight attempt to trace the identity of the Countess, but with little success, and had soon given up the search.

'There is an antiquarian problem for you to solve, Henry,' said he, 'but I don't know where you should look for the solution. The annals of Rosemount are very imperfect. In those within my reach I could find nothing bearing on the subject.'

'I am afraid, sir,' said Henry, 'if you failed I am not likely to succeed, for I am only a very humble antiquary, and should not know where to begin. It seems to me, however, that the story must have had something to do with the history of the Abbey, and that its fortunes were connected with the wicked Countess or the monks would not have put her story in their windows.'

'Well, then, there you have a clue to follow up,' said his uncle, 'and now let us join the ladies.'

The room where Henry Charlton was to sleep was on the ground floor in one corner of the house, and looked out upon the cloister and the ruined abbey-church. It was, as his uncle had said, a relic of the domestic part of the Abbey, and when he had parted with his cousin Charley, who guided him thither, he looked round the apartment with the keenest interest. It was a fair-sized room, low-pitched, with a ceiling of massive black timbers, plastered between the joists. The wall was so thick that there was room for a little seat in the window recess on each side, which was reached by a step, for the window sill was rather high above the floor.

Opposite the window yawned a wide fireplace with dogs for

wood-logs, and a heap of wood ashes lying on the hearth. The walls were panelled with oak up to the ceiling, and the floor, where not covered with rugs, was of the same material polished brightly. But for the toilet appliances of modern civilisation the room was unaltered from the time when the last brother of the convent left it, never to return. Henry tried to picture to himself his predecessor in the apartment; he imagined him sitting at the table, reading or writing, or on his knees in prayer; on his simple shelf would have been his few books and manuscripts, borrowed from the convent library, to which he had to return them when they met in chapter once a year, under severe penalty in case of loss or damage.

As he lay on his bed Henry tried to imagine what his own thoughts would have been had he himself been that ghostly personage five centuries ago; he fancied himself in the choir of the great church; he heard the sonorous Gregorian chanting by a score of deep manly voices, ringing in the vaulted roof, and echoing through the aisles; he saw the embroidered vestments, the lights that shone clearer and brighter as the shades of evening wrapped arcade and triforium in gloom and mystery, and turned to blackness the stories windows that lately gleamed with the hues of the sapphire, the ruby and the emerald. Pleased with these fancies he lay awake till the clock struck twelve and then insensibly the vision faded and he fell asleep.

His sleep was not untroubled. Several times he half awoke, only to drop off again and resume the thread of a tiresome dream that puzzled and worried him but led to no conclusion. When morning came, he woke in earnest, and tried to piece together the fragments he could remember, but made little of them. He seemed to have seen the monk sitting at the table as he had pictured him in imagination the evening before. The monk was not reading but turning over some little bottles which he took from a leathern case, and he seemed to be waiting for someone or something.

Then Henry in his dream fancied that someone did come and something did happen, but what it was he could not remember, and of the visitor he could recall nothing, except that he felt there was a personality present, but not so as to be seen and recognised; more an impression than a fact. He could remember, however, a hand stretched out towards the seated figure and the objects he was handling. More than this he could not distinctly recall, but the same figures recurred each time he fell asleep with slightly varied attitude, though with no greater distinctness. For the monk he could account by the thoughts that had been in his mind the night before, but for the incident in his dream, if so vague a matter could be called an incident, he could trace no suggestion in his mind.

The bright summer morning and the merry party at breakfast soon drove the memory of the dream out of his head. After breakfast there were the horses and dogs to be seen, and the garden to be visited, and it was not till the afternoon that his cousins let him satisfy his longing to visit the ruins of the church and cloister. There they all went in a body. The cloister lawn was mown smoothly and well tended, and here and there barely rising above the green sward were the stones that marked the resting places of the brotherhood.

Part of the cloister retained its traceried windows and vaulted roof, and on the walls were inscribed the names of abbots and monks whose bones lay beneath the pavement. At the end of the western walk a finely sculptured door led into the nave of the church, the oldest part of the building, built when the ruder Norman work was just melting into greater refinement. Henry was in raptures, and vowed that neither Fountains nor Rievaulx could show anything more perfect. The girls were delighted to find their favourite parts of the building appreciated, and led him from point to point, determined that he should miss nothing.

'And now,' said Cissy, 'you have to see the best bit of all, hasn't he, Kate? We don't show it to everybody for fear strangers might do mischief.'

So saying she pushed open a door in the side wall and led them into a chantry chapel built out between two of the great

15

buttresses of the nave aisle. It was indeed a gem of architecture of the purest fourteenth-century Gothic and Henry stood entranced at its loveliness. The delicate traceries on wall and roof were carved with the finish of ivory, and though somewhat stained by weather, for the windows had lost their glass, had kept all their sharp precision. Part of the outer wall had given way, weeds and ivy had invaded and partly covered the floor, and a thick mass of vegetation was piled up under the windows against the masonry.

'What a pity to let this lovely place get into such a mess,' said Henry.' I have never seen anything more beautiful.'

'Well,' said Charley, 'it wouldn't take long to clear all this rubbish away. Suppose we set to work and do it?'

So while the girls sat and looked on, the two men fetched some garden tools, and cut, hacked and pulled up weeds and ivy and brambles, which they threw out by the breach in the wall, and soon made a partial clearance. Henry had begun on the mass that stood breast-high next the window, when a sudden exclamation made the others look at him. He was peering down into the mass of vegetation, of which he had removed the top layer, with an expression of amazement that drew the others to his side.

Looking up at them out of the mass of ivy was a face, the face of a beautiful woman, her hair disposed in graceful masses, and bound by a slender coronet. It was evident that under the pile of vegetation was a tomb with an effigy that had long been hidden, and the very existence of which had been forgotten. When the rest of the vegetation had been cleared away there appeared an altar tomb on the top of which lay the alabaster figure of a woman. The sides bore escutcheons of heraldry and had evidently once been coloured.

The figure was exquisitely modelled, the work of no mean sculptor; the hands were crossed on the breast, and the drapery magnificently composed. But with the head of the figure the artist had surpassed himself. It was a triumph of sculpture. The features were of perfect beauty, something akin to life, something that seemed to respond to the gaze of the observer, and to attract him unconsciously whether he would or not. The group of discoverers hung over it in a sort of fascination for some minutes saying nothing.

At last Kate, the elder girl, drew back with a slight shiver, and said 'Oh! What is it, what is the matter with me, I feel as if there was something wrong; it is too beautiful; I don't like it; come away, Cissy,' and she drew her sister out of the chapel, in a sort of tremor.

Charley followed them, and Henry was left alone with his gaze still fixed on the lovely face. As he looked he seemed to read fresh meaning in the cold alabaster features. The mouth, though perfectly composed in rest, appeared to express a certain covert satire. The eyes were represented as open, and they seemed to regard him with a sort of amused curiosity.

There was a kind of diablerie about the whole figure. It was a long time before he could remove his eyes from the face that seemed to understand and return his gaze, and it was not without a wrench that at last he turned away. The features of the image seemed to be burned into his brain, and to remain fixed there indelibly, whether pleasurably or not he could not decide, for mixed with a strange attraction and even fascination he was conscious of an undercurrent of terror, and even of aversion, as from something unclean. As he moved away, his eye caught an inscription in Gothic lettering round the edge of the slab on which the figure lay.

*HIC JACET ALIANORA COMITISSA PECCATRIX*
*QVÆ OBIT ANO DNI MCCCL CVIVS ANIMÆ*
*MISEREATVR DEVS*

He copied the epitaph in his notebook, remarking that it differed from the usual formula, and then closing the door of the chantry he followed his cousins back to the house.

'Well, here you are at last,' said Lady Wilmot, as Charley and his sisters emerged on the lawn.

'What a time you have been in the ruins, and the tea is getting cold. And what have you done with Henry?'

'Oh, mother,' cried Crissy, 'we have had such an adventure. You know that little chantry chapel we are so fond of; well, we thought it wanted tidying up, and so we cleared away the weeds and rubbish, and what do you think we found? Why, the most lovely statue you ever saw, and we left Henry looking at it as if he had fallen in love with it and could not tear himself away.'

'By Jove!' said Charley, 'just like old Pygmalion, who fell in love with a statue and got Venus to bring it to life for him.'

'Don't talk so, Charley,' said Kate, 'I am sure I don't want this stone lady to come to life. There is something uncanny about her, I can't describe what, but was very glad to get away from her.'

'Yes, mother,' said Cissy, 'Kate was quite frightened of the stone lady and dragged me away, just as I was longing to look at her, for you never saw anything so lovely in your life.'

'But there is one thing I noticed, father,' said Charley, 'that I think wants looking to. I noticed a bad crack in that fine vault over the chantry which looks dangerous, and I think Parsons should be sent to have a look at it.'

'Thank you, Charley,' said Sir Thomas, 'I should be sorry if anything happened to that part of the building, foe archaeologists tell me it's the most perfect thing of its kind in England. Parsons is busy on other matters for the next few days, but I will have it seen to next week. By the way, we shall have another visitor tonight. You remember Henry's college friend, Mr. Edwards; I heard he was staying at the Johnstons and so I asked him to come here for a few days while Henry is with us, and here I think he comes across the lawn.'

Edwards had some previous acquaintance with the Wilmots, and was soon set down to tea with the rest, and engaged for lawn tennis afterwards, a game in which he had earned a great reputation.

Henry Charlton did not appear till the party were assembled in the drawing-room before dinner. On leaving the Abbey he was possessed by a disinclination for the lively society on the lawn. His nerves were in a strange flutter; he felt as if something unusual was impending, as if he had passed a barrier and shut the gate behind him, and had entered on a new life where strange experiences awaited him. He could not account for it. He tried to dismiss the finding of the statue as a mere antiquarian discovery, interesting both in history and in art; but it would not do.

That face, with its enigmatical expression, haunted him, and would not be dismissed. He felt that this was not the end of the adventure; that in some mysterious way the dead woman of five centuries back had touched his life, and that more would come of it. To that something more he looked forward with the same indefinable mixture of attraction and repulsion which he had felt in the chapel while gazing at those pure alabaster features.

He must be alone. He could not at present come back to the converse of ordinary life, and he set off on a swinging walk through field and woodland to try and steady his nerves, so as to meet his friends in the evening with composure. A good ten-mile stretch did something to restore him to his usual spirits. He was pleased to find his friend Edwards, of whose coming he had been told, and when he took his place at the dinner table next to his aunt there was nothing unusual in his manner.

The conversation during dinner naturally turned on the discovery that had been made in the Abbey that afternoon. It was singular that so remarkable a work of art should have been forgotten, and been overlooked by the Northampton Archaeological Society, which had so many enthusiastic antiquaries in its ranks. There had been meetings of the society in the ruins, papers about them had been read and published, plans had been made and illustrations drawn of various parts of the building, including the chantry itself, but there was no mention or indication given of the monument either in the text or in the plates. Strange that no one should ever have thought of looking into that tangle of brambles by which it was concealed, till that very day.

'I must go first thing tomorrow,' said Sir Thomas, 'to see your wonderful discovery. The next thing will be to find out who this pretty lady was.'

'That I think I can tell you, sir,' said Henry, who now spoke for almost the first time, 'and I think it helps to solve the mystery of the sinful Countess in the painted windows opposite, which puzzled us last night.'

All eyes turned to the fragments of painted glass in the hall windows, as Henry continued.

'You see in the first window the devil is tempting the Countess ALI— the rest of her name being lost. Well, on the tomb is an epitaph, which gives the missing part. She is the Countess Alianora; no doubt as the lady whose adventures were depicted in the windows.'

'Now I know,' broke in Kate, 'why I was frightened in the chapel. She was a wicked woman, and something told me so, and made me want to go away from her.'

'Well,' said Lady Wilmot, 'let us hope she mended her ways and ended her life well. You see she went to Rome and was absolved by the Pope.'

'Yes, but I bet she did not get absolution for nothing,' said Charley. 'Just look at her in the last picture and you will see she has a church in her hand. Depend on it, she got her wicked deeds pardoned in return for her gifts to Rosemount Abbey; and I daresay she rebuilt a great part of it and among the rest her own charity.'

'Charley,' said Edwards, 'you ought to be a lawyer; you make out such a good case for the prosecution.'

'At all events,' said Sir Thomas, 'Charley gives us a good lead for our research. I will look out the old deeds and try to find out what connection, if any, there was between Rosemount Abbey and a Countess Alianora of some place unknown.'

The rest of the evening passed in the usual way. A few friends from neighbouring houses joined the party; there was a little impromptu dancing, and it was near midnight by the time they retired to rest. Henry had enjoyed himself like the rest, and forgot the adventure of the afternoon till he found himself once more alone in the monastic cell, looking out on the ruined

Abbey. The recollection of his dream of the night before then for the first time recurred to him; he wondered whether it had any connection with his later experience in the chantry, but he could trace none whatever. The dream seemed merely one of those fanciful imaginings with which we are all familiar, devoid of any further meaning.

He was not, however, destined to repose quietly. This time his dream showed him the same monk, he recognised him by his coarse features and shaggy brows, but he was in the nave of a church, and in the massive round pillars and severe architecture of the arches and triforium, Henry knew the nave of Rosemount Abbey, not as now, in ruins, but vaulted and entire. It was nearly dark, and the choir behind the pulpitum was wrapped in gloom, in the midst of which twinkled a few lights before the high altar and the various saintly shrines. The monk held something small in his hand, and was evidently, as on the night before, waiting for somebody or something.

At last Henry was aware that somebody had indeed come. A shadowy figure draped in black moved swiftly out from behind a pillar and approached the monk. What the figure was he tried in vain to discover. All he could see was that just as had happened on the night before a hand was stretched out and took something from the monk, which it promptly hid in the drapery with which the face was covered. The hand, however, was more clearly seen this time. It was a woman's hand, white and delicate, and a jewel sparkled on her finger. The scene caused Henry a dull terror, as of some unknown calamity, or as of some crime that he had witnessed, and he woke with a start and found himself in a cold sweat.

He got up and paced his apartment to and fro, and then looked out of the window. It was brilliant moonlight, throwing strong shadows of the broken walls across the quiet cloister garth where the monks of old lay quietly sleeping till the last dread summons should awake them. The light fell full on the nave walls

*Where buttress and buttress alternately*

and the light touched with the magic of mystery the delicate traceries of the chantry where lay the Countess Alianora. Her face flashed upon his memory, with its enigmatical expression, half attracting, half repelling, and an irresistible desire impelled him to see her again. His window was open and the ground only a few feet below. He dressed himself hastily and clambered out. Everything was still; all nature seemed asleep, not a breath of wind moved the trees or stirred the grass as he slowly passed along the cloister: his mind was in a strange state of nervous excitement; he was almost in a trance as he advanced into the nave where the shadows of column and arch fell black on the broken pavement.

He paused for a moment at the gate which led into the chantry, and then entered as if in a dream, for everything seemed to him unreal, and he himself a mere phantom. At last he stood beside the tomb and looked down on the lovely countenance which had bewitched him in the afternoon. The moonlight fell upon it, investing it with an unearthly mystery and charm. Its beauty was indescribable: never had he conceived anything so lovely. The strange semi-satirical expression of which he had been conscious in the afternoon had disappeared; nothing could be read in the features but sweetness and allurement. A passionate impulse seized him, and he bent down and kissed her on the lips. Was it fancy or was it real, that soft lips of warm life seemed to meet his own? He knew not: a delirious ecstasy transported him, the scene faded before his eyes and he sank on the floor in a swoon.

How long he lay he never knew. When he came to himself the moon had sat, and he was in darkness. An indefinable terror seized him. He struggled to his feet, burst out of the Abbey, fled to his rooms, scrambling in through the window, and threw himself panting on his bed.

Henry Charlton was the last to appear next morning at the breakfast-table. He was pale and out of spirits, and roused himself with difficulty to take part in the discussion as to what was to be done that day. After breakfast he pleaded a headache, and retired with a book to the library, while the others betook themselves to various amusements or employments. The girls were in the garden where they found old Donald the gardener, whose life had been spent at Rosemount, and in whose eyes the garden was as much his as his master's, and perhaps more so.

'Yes, missy,' he was saying, 'the weeds do grow terrible this fine weather, and as you was saying it is time we cleaned up a bit in the old Abbey. But I see the young gentlemen has been doing a bit theirselves, chucking all them briars and rubbish out on the grass just as I had mown and tidied it.'

'Why Donald,' said Cissy, 'you ought to have thanked them, for that chapel was in an awful mess, and they have saved you some trouble.'

'Well, miss, I suppose they pleased theirselves, but that's not where I should have meddled, no, no!' and so saying he moved away.

'But why not there,' said Kate, 'why not there of all places?'

'Oh! I say nothing about it,' said Donald, 'Only folk do say that there's them there as don't like to be disturbed.'

'Indeed; what do they say in the village about it?'

'Oh! Ay! I say nothing. I don't meddle with things above me. And I shan't tell ye any more, miss, it's not good for young women to know.'

'But do you know Donald,' said Cissy, 'what we found there?'

'What did you find, miss? Not her? Oh, Lord! She was found once before, and no good come of it. There, don't ask me anymore about it. It's not good for young women to know.' So saying Donald wheeled his barrow away into another part of the garden.

'Father,' said Kate, to Sir Thomas who now came up. 'Donald knows all about the tomb and the statue, and he won't tell us anything, except that the people think it unlucky to meddle with it. Have you ever heard of any superstition about it?'

'Nothing at all,' said he. 'I have just been down to look at your discovery. The statue is a wonderful piece of work. I have never seen anything finer either here or in Italy. But the chapel is in a bad way and part of the roof threatens to fall. I have just sent word to Parsons to come tomorrow morning and attend to it.'

They were joined presently by Edwards and Charley, and the day passed pleasantly enough, with the usual amusements of a country house in holiday time. Henry did not take much part with them. He was abstracted and inattentive, and altogether out of spirits. He had but a confused idea of what had happened the previous night, but there seemed still to linger on his lips that mystic, perhaps unhallowed kiss, and there still floated before his eyes the mocking enigma of that lovely countenance. He dreaded the approach of night, not knowing what it might bring, and did his best to divert his mind to other things, but without success.

His friend Edwards was much concerned at the change in his behaviour, and asked Charley whether Henry had been upset in any way during his visit. He was assured that till yesterday afternoon Henry had been as happy and as companionable as possible, and that it was only that morning the change had come over him.

'But I can tell you one thing,' said Charley, 'I believe he was out of his room last night, for the flower beds show footmarks, and the creepers are torn outside his window, showing someone had been getting in and out, and there certainly has been no burglary in the house. Do you know whether he walks in his sleep?'

'I have never heard that he does,' said Edwards. 'We can't very well ask him whether anything is wrong, for he does not seem to invite inquiry, and has rather avoided us all day. But if it is a case of sleep-walking we might perhaps keep a lookout tonight to prevent his coming to mischief.'

'All right,' said Charley. 'My room is over his and looks out the same way. I'll try and keep awake till midnight, and will call you if I see anything of him.'

'That's well,' said Edwards, 'but we must be careful and not be seen, for it is dangerous to wake a somnambulist I believe.'

And so they departed to their several chambers.

The first part of the night passed peacefully enough with Henry. He had no dreams to trouble him, but towards midnight he began to turn uneasily in his bed, and to be oppressed by an uneasy feeling that he was not alone. He awoke to find the moon shining as brilliantly as on the previous night, and bringing into view every detail of the ancient buildings opposite. A dull sense of some sinister influence weighed upon him: someone was with him whom he could not see, whispering in his ear, '*You are mine; you are mine.*'

He could see no form, but to his mental vision was clearly visible the countenance of the figure in the chapel, now with the satirical, mocking expression more fully shown, and he felt himself drawn on he knew not whither. Again the mocking lips seemed to say, '*You are mine, you are mine.*' Half unconsciously he rose from his bed, and advanced towards the window.

A faintly visible form seemed to move before him, he saw the features of the countess more plainly, and without knowing how he got there he found himself outside the room in the cloister garth, and entering the shade of the cloister. Something impalpable glided on before him, turning on him the face that attracted him though it mocked him and which he could not but follow, though with an increasing feeling of terror and dislike.

Still on his ear feel the words, '*You are mine, you are mine,*' and he was helpless to resist the spell that drew him on and on farther into the gloom of the ruined nave. And now the shape gathered consistency and he seemed to see the Countess Alianora standing facing him. On her features the same mocking smile, on her finger the jewel of his dream.

'*You are mine,*' she seemed to say, '*mine, mine, you sealed it with a kiss,*' and she outstretched her arms; but as she stood before him in her marvellous and unearthly beauty, a change came over her; her face sank into ghastly furrows, her limbs shrivelled, and as she advanced upon him, a mass of loathly corruption, and stretched out her horrible arms to embrace him he uttered a dreadful scream as of a soul in torture, and sank fainting on the ground.

'Edwards, Edwards, come quick,' cried Charley, beating at his door. 'Henry is out of his room, and there is something with him, I don't know what it is, but hurry up or some mischief may happen.'

His friend was ready in a moment, and the two crept cautiously downstairs, and as the readiest way, not to disturb the household, got out into the cloister through the window of Henry's room. They noticed on the way that his bed had been slept in, and was tossed about in disorder. They took the way of the cloister by which Charley had seen Henry go, and had just reached the door that led into the nave when his unearthly scream of terror fell on their ears. They rushed into the church, crying, 'Henry, Henry, here we are what is it, where are you?' and having no reply they searched as well as they could in the moonlight.

They found him at last, stretched on the ground at the entrance to the fatal chantry chapel. At first they thought he was dead, but his pulse beat faintly, and they carried him out, still insensible, into the outer air. He showed some signs of life before long, but remained unconscious. The house was aroused and he was put to bed, and messengers were sent for the doctor. As they watched by his bedside, a thundering crash startled them; looking out of the window they saw a cloud of dust where the chantry had been, and next morning it was seen that the roof had fallen in, and destroyed it.

Henry Charlton lay many weeks with a brain fever. From his cries and ravings something was gathered of the horrors of that fatal night, but he would never be induced to tell the whole story after he recovered.

The fallen ruin was removed, and Sir Thomas hoped that the beautiful statue might have escaped. But strange to say, though every fragment of masonry was carefully examined and accounted for, no trace could be found of any alabaster figure nor of the tomb of Comitissa Alianora.

# The Ring

Two Englishmen were sitting one autumn evening in the garden of the inn at Corneto. The sun had just set over the sea, and the short Italian twilight had begun. The plain down below was already in shadow, but hues of purple and violet still tinged the hills, and invested them with all the ineffable charm of a Tuscan landscape at eventide. The elder of the two men was an Oxford Don, a well-known antiquary and student of ethnology. The younger had been a fellow of the same college, but had settled in London and taken to literary pursuits, in which he had already made his mark. They had spent the morning in the museum, examining with the help of the courteous curator the rich collection of Etruscan antiquities, and in the afternoon had visited the famous necropolis on the plateau behind the town, and penetrated into a score or more of the painted tombs.

They finished the day by crossing the valley to the bare plateau on the opposite hill, where once stood the proud city of Tarquinii, which gave kings to Rome, when Rome itself was but a thing of yesterday, sprung from an upstart settlement of outlaws and robbers. As they sat and sipped their coffee in the gathering dusk, their minds were full of what they had seen; of the mystery of that strange people who had come to Italy from nobody knows where, whose written language nobody had ever interpreted, whose gloomy religion coloured the whole ritual of the Romans, and of whom the best record is to be found in their graves.

"I can imagine nothing more delightful," said the younger man at last, "than to penetrate into an untouched Etruscan tomb, another Regulini-Galassi discovery; where, though the body may have turned to dust—though, for the matter of that, glimpses have been seen of one before it fell to pieces—the ornaments that had fallen off show how the man lay amid the votive offerings to his gods, with his cherished possessions and trinkets all standing around him or hanging on the walls just as they had been left by his relatives three thousand years ago. But I fear there is no chance of such a piece of luck nowadays. The tombs everywhere seem either to have been rifled in bygone ages, or stripped in modern times, to enrich the museums and collections."

"Well, I don't know," said Dr. Morton, the elder man; "it may be, as you say, too late for discovery, and yet—But at all events, I agree with you that nothing could be more interesting."

"You were here some weeks before I joined you," said Archie Bryant. "I think mainly you came to study the folk-lore of Tuscan peasantry. How have you been rewarded?"

"Fairly well. It is not easy to get below the surface with the Italian peasant when you try to fathom his beliefs. But it is curious how much has survived of something older than the Catholic faith he shows to his priest."

"Indeed," said Bryant. "Do you mean he has not forgotten Tinia, Farfluns, and Teramo, and the other Etruscan deities whom we have been looking at on vases, and in the tombs?"

"So far from having forgotten them," said Morton, "many of the old peasants, though they are Catholics outwardly, have much more real faith in *la vecchia religione,* the outworn creed, as you would think it, of Etruscan mythology. There are still many women *streghe,* witches, who know, and practise incantations, but of course all that is under the ban of the Church, and though luckily the Holy Office can no longer burn them, they are very timid and afraid of attracting notice. However, I have managed to get into the confidence of some of them, and have learned a good deal that would surprise you, as it certainly did me. It is even said that it is usual for a family to have one of their number brought up in the old religion, in order that they may have friends in all quarters."

Bryant laughed, and said it was like the way families in the time of the Wars of the Roses took care to have some of their relatives in each camp, so as to have a friend on either side in case of accidents.

"But to return to what you said just now," said Morton, "about visiting an untouched Etruscan tomb, do you know that I have got great hopes we may really manage it. One of the women into whose confidence I have got, and who has given me a host of spells and incantations which I hope someday to publish, is a *strega*, or witch, and my belief is that she knows of such a tomb. She says, however, it is dangerous to visit it, no doubt from some superstitious views about the old gods—Tinia, the god of thunder, and the rest. But we shall know more tomorrow, and I have no doubt we shall manage to open the tomb with the aid of a golden key."

They laughed, and rose from their seats, and, after a turn or two in the alleys of the garden, went to bed.

The next morning was spent partly in the museum, and partly in the communal library. Bryant's interest was excited by the subject of Etruscan mythology, which was new to him, and under Morton's guidance he dipped into the ample stores of literature that bore upon it. As they walked away in the evening Bryant said:

"And you really mean to tell me that Tinia and other members of the old Etruscan Olympus still have their followers among the descendants of the people whose tombs we have visited. I can hardly believe it."

"I don't wonder you should be incredulous," replied Morton. "They do not have it all to themselves, for the saints have their share of popular favour; but, besides the prayers that they offer to the saints, many of the peasants believe in the *folletti* or spirits of the past; charms and incantations are addressed to them, and legends are preserved of their potent aid. But in a few minutes

I will convince you beyond all doubt. We are going to visit an acquaintance I have made—the woman of whom I told you last night; and there she is waiting for me. I doubt, by the way, whether she is actually one of the *streghe*, or witches, but she knows most of their lore."

Bryant saw a peasant woman seated at her door, spinning with distaff and spindle as her ancestors had done before her from time immemorial. She rose at their approach, pushed the end of the distaff through her belt, and greeted them with a dignified curtsey that sits naturally on the Italian of the humblest degree, his heritage from an ancient civilisation. She seemed to Bryant a woman of sixty years, or perhaps younger, for women age more rapidly in Italy than with us, and she retained much of the classic beauty of her youth.

"Antonietta," said Morton, "I have brought a compatriot, a lover of your country and people."

"The *Signore* is welcome," said Antonietta, with a smile and a slight inclination, and she invited them to enter her house. A young girl who was sitting there rose as they entered, whom Antonietta presented as her daughter Chiarina. She was a Tuscan beauty, with blue eyes and a rich complexion burned by the sun to a tint like the bloom on an apricot, set off by the bright-coloured handkerchief thrown over her head and fastened with silver pins.

"I have been telling my friend," said Morton, "what you told me the other day of a tomb which—"

"Ah!" said Antonietta, interrupting him. "*Scusi, Signore.* These things must not be spoken of lightly," and she looked furtively round and shut the door carefully. Returning to Morton's side, she continued in a low voice:

"And is the *Signore* really bent on what he proposed? Is he not afraid of disturbing those we dare not speak of?"

"We should make no disturbance, Antonietta," said he. "I only want to see a tomb of one of the old people just as it was finished and left by those who made it. I think you said you knew of one that had never been disturbed."

"There is such a tomb, *Signore*, and Chiarina knows it as well as I. No one else does. But it is dangerous for strangers to visit it, as I have warned you, *Signore*."

"But you and Chiarina go there safely," said Morton.

"Yes, but that is different. There are reasons," and she nodded her head sagely. "We are known. They would not harm us."

"Is that why you wear a guard against evil spirits?" said Bryant, pointing to the silver cross that hung on her bosom. "They cannot touch a good Catholic, I suppose."

"*Si, si, sicuro; sono buona Cattolica*," replied Antonietta. "I am a good Catholic, though I do not believe all the priest tell me." And then in a lower voice to Morton, "*You know* what I believe."

"*La vecchia religione*, the old religion," said Morton. She nodded two or three times, but said nothing.

"But now about this tomb," said Morton, returning to the object of his visit.

"*Signore*, be advised. Think no more about it. There are those there who would not welcome you. It would not be wholesome for you to go. I speak for your good."

"But I will be careful to give no offence," said Morton. "I am bent on going, and trust to you to help me," and as he spoke he slipped two gold pieces into her hand. Antonietta looked at them for a minute, and then said:

"Well, if the *Signore* is resolved, I can certainly guide him, but, no! I will not be paid for it," and she laid the money down on the table and pushed it towards him. "Neither dare I take you myself. Chiarina knows the way, and she is not bound like me. She shall take you, but it must be by night and secretly, and there must be no more than you two."

Morton faithfully promised to obey her conditions, and it was arranged that Chiarina should meet them after dark at the town gate which gave on to the necropolis.

They were punctual at the rendezvous, and found Chiarina waiting for them. She was dressed in black, and had a black shawl or hood over her head which concealed her features. She made a sign of recognition, and preceded them without a word.

It was a lovely starlit night, without a moon. Not a breath of air stirred the trees, and the silence was unbroken save by the silver tone of the bell on the Palazzo Comunale, tolling the hour of twenty-three. A few belated wanderers returning to the city passed them on the high road, but as their footsteps died away in the distance, the dead silence settled down again. When they had proceeded about a mile Chiarina turned off by a by-path, that led across the solitary waste. Around them lay the unseen city of the dead; the ground was honeycombed with tombs, where, amid pictured scenes of dancing and revelry, a mockery as it were of mortality, lay the dust of Lucomos and warriors, people of that mysterious race whose history and language are alike forgotten.

"And yet," said Morton, "one may believe that they are the same people still; mixed, no doubt, with Goths and Lombards, but mainly derived from the old stock that worshipped Tinia here before the days of Romulus."

"I like the idea," said Bryant, "and, according to you, they still pay him a divided homage, though he has many rivals in Catholic hagiology. But I like to think that Chianira's ancestors followed Lars Porsena of Clusium to the siege of Rome—"

Their guide caught the mention of her name, and looked round with her finger on her lip to enjoin silence. They were traversing through a thick wood of under growth by a path obscurely marked, which might easily be overlooked by one who was not familiar with the route, but Chiarina never faltered or hesitated on her way. They now descended slightly into thicker grove; the trees met overhead, and it was with difficulty they saw their guide before them.

At last she stopped and turned to her companions. Taking Morton by the hand and signing to Bryant to follow, she drew them through a thicket and then, striking a match, lighted one of the earthen lamps that the peasants still use, exactly like those found in the tombs of their ancestors and placed there three thousand years ago. They found themselves facing a ledge of rocks, about ten feet high, that had evidently been scarped by the band of man to a smooth face.

Here Chiarina turned to them, and in a whisper warned them to be silent.

"The *Signori* will be so good," she said, "as not to speak while we are here. There are those whom we must not disturb, or they will be angry. But I will do what is wanted to appease them."

They promised to do as she bid them, Bryant much interested in her seriousness and her unfeigned alarm, and amused at the idea of two prosaic Englishmen in the twentieth century assisting in a religious function of thirty centuries ago.

Pulling away a bundle of brushwood, Chiarina showed by the feeble light of her lamp a descent of steep steps leading to a doorway at the foot of the rock, and following her they entered an excavation imperfectly visible till their eyes had become more accustomed to the darkness. They then found themselves in a vaulted chamber, cut in the rock, with a square pier left in the middle to support the roof.

On this pillar, as Chiarina held her lamp high above her head, they saw a huge figure of Typhon, with twisted serpents for legs, and outstretched wings, grasping a thunderbolt as if to hurl it at an intruder. The walls presented to their delighted eyes a series of paintings as perfect as when the artist had given them his last touches. On one side were rural scenes, harvest and vintage, with jocund peasants and oxen. On another were pictures of banquet and revelry, youths piping and maidens dancing. All spoke of the joy of life, of nature, and contentment. On another wall were scenes more appropriate to the place: there sat Hades black and gloomy, and beside him Persephone with snakes bound in her hair. While Charon, *con occhi di bra gia,* with his bark stood awaiting his freight of souls. All this, however, was like what the visitors had seen in other tombs during the preceding day, though nowhere so brilliantly preserved as here.

But what was their wonder to see around them the treasury of the dead, untouched by the hand of man since the last inmate of the tomb had been laid to rest. His golden collar and breastplate and other ornaments lay on a bier of bronze, though the body that wore them had melted away from within them into dust. On the wall hung his weapons, and around were arranged painted vases, such as form the priceless treasures of countless museums. Morton and Bryant had indeed their wish satisfied to the full.

As they stood in the death-like silence of the tomb, the mystery of the ages weighed upon their senses; the unknown occupant whose dust undisturbed no doubt lay still on the floor: the things he had used in life, that had hung idly beside his bier for countless centuries; the inscriptions on the walls intended to tell who and what he had been, which could be read but which no one could understand, all combined to make indescribable impression on the imagination. Pictures of the gods of the outworn creed of ancient Etruria surrounded them—outworn, but no! What was Chiarina doing? At the far end of the cell she had lighted a little flame on a bronze tripod, and while dropping on it pinches of incense, was muttering some charm or incantation of which only a few words reached them. The ancient deities, then, still had their worshippers.

As Bryant looked on in amazement, a strange sense of unreality clouded his mind: he was for the moment as it were transported back to ancient days, the present was confused with the past, and the intervening centuries vanished as in a dream. Before he recovered himself something fell on his foot. He stooped to pick it up. It was a ring. And he half-unconsciously put it on his finger.

As he rose he met the gaze of the Typhon painted on the central pillar. In the flickering light of the lamp it seemed instinct with life; its expression seemed changed, and it appeared to regard him with malevolence and deadly hate. Its gaze fascinated him, and he could not remove his eyes till the touch of Morton on his elbow recalled him to himself, and he saw that Chiarina had finished her divinations and was anxiously urging them to depart. As they mounted the steps that led to the upper world, a vivid flash of lightning was followed almost instantaneously by the crash of thunder. Chiarina clung to them in terror.

"Go, go, *Signori*," cried she. "It is Tinia. He is angry. I must go back to appease him," and she pushed them through the thicket into the pathway and then disappeared into the darkness. Left without a guide, they scrambled as best they could through the wood and open into the open country, and with some trouble found the high road. A few lights of the town twinkled in the distance to direct them, and they hurried onward with a strange sense of insecurity. The heavens were black with clouds, the lightning was incessant, a deluge of rain caught them while they were still in the open, and they arrived at the inn drenched to the skin.

"A strange adventure," muttered Morton as they parted for the night. "A trifle uncanny, eh? One might almost imagine there was after all something in their creed, were it not too absurd. But what is that on your finger?"

Bryant looked at his hand. He had forgotten the ring he picked up, and he now examined it with curiosity. It was a curious piece of Etruscan goldsmith's work with some letters inscribed round the rim which he could not decipher.

"Oh! The ring," said he. "It fell at my feet from somewhere or other. I suppose I brushed against one of the bronze tables and knocked it off, and I picked it up and slipped it on my finger, and then forgot all about it."

"H'm! Well, you know best," said Morton, "but I think you would have done better to have left it there. However, goodnight, I am longing to get dry again."

Bryant was of an imaginative turn of mind, as befitted his literary vocation, and the adventure of the night made an impression on him that kept him for some time awake. The whole scene presented itself to his memory; the silent walk, the wood, the mysterious tomb with its contents, and above all the countenance of the Typhon with its scowl of concentrated hate. This last pursued him into dreamland, and caused him to pass a troubled night.

Next morning they thought it right to go and see whether

their young guide had got safely back, and had not suffered from the storm. Chiarina, however, it appeared had fared better then they, for the storm ceased about the time they reached Corneto. But Antonietta was anxious and troubled. Something she said was wrong, and the storm showed displeasure on the part of the powers on whom they had intruded. As they were leaving Corneto that afternoon, Morton shook her by the hand, and said, "You see, Antonietta, no harm but a wetting has come of our visit, which you thought so dangerous."

Antonietta said nothing, but when Bryant offered his hand her eye caught sight of the ring. Dropping his hand she made an exclamation of horror.

"*Signore*," she cried, "do you know what you have done, you have brought a curse upon you; restore the ring at once, or mischief will befall you."

"But we are leaving Corneto today," said Morton, "and have no time for another visit. And what harm can come of a ring?"

"Besides," said Bryant, "on further looking at it, I think it is a very curious piece of work; and I mean to give it to the Museum when I get home."

"If you keep it," said Antonietta in great excitement, "perhaps you will not get home. And you will never give it to the Museum, for it will not leave you till you restore it to the place you took it from. The hand that took must be the hand to restore."

"But that is impossible," said they both. There was no time to go back to the tomb. And besides Bryant had taken a fancy to it, and looked forward to presenting the Museum with a genuine antique, of whose authenticity there could be no question. He even declined to give it to Antonietta who said she herself would take it back, and that would suffice. At last she threw up her hands in despair, and retreating into her cottage slammed the door behind her.

Early in the afternoon they parted; Morton for Rome, and Bryant for Viterbo, by way of Toscanella where he meant to stay a day or two to see the two fine churches, and the Etruscan tombs. His conveyance was a primitive cat little better than a costermonger's cart, drawn by a weedy little horse, and driven by a hobblehoy of a lad, the son of the proprietor. The road at first lay along the high plateau where the tombs were. In the country beyond there were no houses or villages to be seen, through the land was well cultivated, for the farmers and their men go in and out daily in carts from the town.

The desolate country had been the scene of brigandage not long before, and the memory of Tiburzi and his nephew was not yet extinct. Giovanni amused Bryant with tales of this sordid hero, and of his escapes, and final capture, till their conversation was suddenly stopped by a lurch of the vehicle which threw them both into the ditch.

On getting to their feet they found that beyond a few bruises and scratches, neither of them was hurt, but the cart had one wheel off, and the shaft broken. They were at least seven miles from Corneto, and more from Toscanella; there was no place nearer where help could be had, and they were in a bad case. At last they decided the only thing was to get back to Corneto. The ruined car they pulled into the ditch, and with cords from the harness secured Bryant's slender luggage on the back of the horse, and set off on foot to retrace their way to Corneto.

Their return caused no little surprise. It was too late to make a fresh start that day, and Bryant returned to his old quarters. As he was undressing his eye caught the ring. Well, thought he, "if Antonietta knew of this accident it would give her a fine argument for her theory that the ring would bring me bad luck."

The loss of a day made Toscanella and Viterbo out of the question, for Bryant had to hurry back to London to complete a magazine article which was wanted by a certain date. Next day therefore, he took the train to Pisa and Genoa on his way home to England. He was curiously unlucky. His luggage was delayed at the frontier, and he arrived in Paris with nothing but a hand hag. This kept him three days more, till the missing portmanteau arrived, and he reached London nearly a week later than he had intended.

Other little accidents of less consequence happened, and

combined to cause him some uneasiness. His nights, moreover, were disturbed by dreams. He seemed always to be drawn towards that silent tomb, and to be face to face with the scowling monster on the pillar. A morbid feeling of terror slowly mastered him. He could not shake it off, and gradually the evil countenance began to intrude itself into his thoughts by day. It interrupted his work, and his writing which had been his greatest pleasure became a labour and a burden.

One day it occurred to him that he had not sent that Etruscan ring to the Museum, and he carefully packed it and sent it to the curator with a letter to say he had been fortunate enough to pick up a genuine piece of Etruscan goldsmith's work in Tuscany, and he would be glad if the Museum authorities would accept it for their collection. He took the packet to the post office himself, and on his return found a parcel on his table from his publisher. On opening it, he found it contained the manuscript of the article he had sent since his return from abroad, the one in fact for the sake of dispatching which, he had been so anxious to get home. A letter from the publisher accompanied it. It ran as follows:

Dear Sir,—I regret to say I am obliged to return your article which in its present shape is quite unsuitable for our pages. The subject on which we invited you to write was one on which we had reason to believe you were an authority, but what you send us seems unequal and largely irrelevant. In particular we fail to understand the allusions in which it abounds to Etruscan mythology.

I am, Sir,

Your obedient servant,

The Editor.

"What on earth does this mean," said Bryant to himself. "The man must have got hold of another paper, and confused it with mine."

The paper, however, was his, and on glancing over it he was aghast. "Is it possible I wrote this balderdash," thought he. "I

38

must be going mad," and he pressed his hand to his brow. But there was no mistake about it being his writing, full of literary faults and widely incoherent as it was. The colour rushed to his cheeks as he tore the shameful pages up and tossed them into an article on the *History of the Colony of New Zealand.*

Was he never to get out of his head the memory of that ill-omened visit? And as his mind reverted to the events of the night the scowling visage of the Typhon presented itself to his mental vision. "Is it possible," he thought, "that the ring has some potent force for evil. Well, anyhow, I am rid of it now; and no further harm can come of it."

He slept better that night, and next day decided to go for a long walk in the country in the hope of steadying his shaken nerves. He found an old college friend disposed for an outing, and they took the train to Clandon, and walked over Newlands Corner to St. Martha's chapel, down to Shamley Green, Wonersh, and Bramley, and so home by rail. They dined together at the Oxford and Cambridge Club, and then parted, Bryant to his chambers in the Temple. On his table, he found a packet by registered post. It contained a letter from the Director of the Museum, and a small parcel in cotton wool of which he guessed too well the contents. The letter ran thus:

Dear Sir,—We are much obliged to you for your kind of-fer of the enclosed ring, which we return with our thanks. It appears to us to be one of the clever copies made in Germany of Etruscan antiquities, by which many collectors have been taken in. We venture to express our hope that you were not too heavily mulcted in the purchase.

Your obedient servant,

—, Director.

"Much they know about it," said Bryant bitterly, as he unfolded the packet, and looked at his fatal possession with dismay. The window was open, and in a sudden rage he flung it far and wide into the court , and went to bed.

He felt better next morning, and after breakfast settled down to some literary work that had come in the day before. But it would not do. His mind was confused, and all power of clear expression seemed to have left him. As he was sitting in despair with his head on his hands there was a knock at the door, and Mrs Filcher, the laundress, entered with something in her hand.

"Begging your pardon, Mr. Bryant," she began, "I picked up this 'ere little ring in the court, and seeing as I have noticed it on your finger, I know'd it to be yourn, and so I have brought it up. Thank you, sir, good-morning, sir."

And the good woman sidled out a shilling the richer, but leaving Bryant in an agony of despair. "Can I never shake off this strange oppression?" thought he, as he gazes on the fatal circlet of gold that lay on the table before him. The words of Antonietta came back to his memory: "it will never leave you till you restore it to the place you took it from." It seemed as if it were true. Twice he had tried in vain to get rid of it, and twice it had been restored; that night he would make sure of a riddance. He remained in his rooms till evening in a sort of mental torpor. He could neither eat nor drink.

A creeping horror took possession of him; as he cast his eyes about in the dusk, innocent bookshelves seemed to resolve themselves into sepulchral forms, and in the midst appeared the scowling visage of the Typhon. At last when night fell he took the ring, descended his staircase, and found his way to the Embankment. The tide was up; with all his might he flung the ring into the river, and then sank down on one of the seats. Famished and exhausted he felt more dead than alive, and half fainting, and half asleep, he lost consciousness.

"Now then, wake up," said a gruff voice in his ear, some hours later, while a heavy hand on his shoulder gave him a good shake, and he woke to find the morning breaking, and a burly policeman standing over him. He roused himself, and stood up.

"Beg pardon, sir," said the policeman, seeing he was a gentleman, "bit overcome, sir, was you? Hadn't you better get to your home, sir, 'stead o' lying here? Let me lend you a hand till you've steadied yourself."

Bryant thanked the man who went off contented with half-a-crown, and then tottered back to his chambers, and threw himself on his bed in a fever. As he sank on the pillow he happened to raise his hand. On his finger was the fatal ring. Was it then only a dream that he had flung it into the river? He could not tell. His brain was in awhirl; one thought only beat upon his mind, "it will never leave you till you restore it to the place you took it from."

He rose from his bed resolved to act on the warning. Every attempt to part with it had failed; the Museum would not have it; and it came back mysteriously twice when he had hurled it away in desperation. Antonietta must be right. He would go to Corneto and find her, and she should guide him again to the fatal place which he now wished to heaven he had never seen.

In half an hour he had put up a small bag of his things, and was on his way to Cook's to secure a sleeping-berth in the St. Gothard express. The excitement he had gone through, his fasting the day before, and his sleepless night began to tell on him. He scarcely noticed anything on the journey, and lived as in a dream. At the frontiers he roused himself to pass the customs, and then sank again into a sort of stupor. At Chiasso he felt a thrill at the thought he was again in Italy, and nearing his point. At Milan there was a delay of some hours which put him in a fever of impatience.

Another night in the train, and then, thank Heaven, in the early morning he alighted at Corneto. He was so weak he could hardly stand, but he managed to reach the omnibus, in which he climbed the hill to the city which is some two miles or do from the station.

He was greeted as an old acquaintance by the *padrone* of the inn where he and Morton had stayed before, to whom he had telegraphed for a room. Breakfast and a bath restored him a little, and then he set off to find Antonietta. He found his way to her house without difficulty, and saw the familiar figure standing at the door and spinning with distaff and spindle as of old.

"Antonietta," he cried, "I am here again, and want your

help."

The woman turned and faced him. It was not Antonietta.

Bryant stood amazed and confounded; the disappointment was too great.

"The *Signore* asked for Antonietta," said she. "Perhaps the *Signore* knew Antonietta."

"Yes, yes," stammered he, "I knew her. Where is she? I am come from England expressly to see her."

"Ah! *Signore*, you have not heard. *La povera Antonietta é morta.* She is dead."

Bryant recovered himself a little, and said:

"And her daughter, Chiarina, is she dead too?"

"Oh, no! *La* Chiarina is well, but she is not here. She is with her friends at Montefiascone. I can give you her address if you like."

Bryant seized on this suggestion with the eagerness of a drowning man grasping at a floating spar, and after resting a little longer at the invitation of the good woman, he rose and managed to regain his hotel. He wrote at once to the address that had been given him, but he could not wait for the answer, and ill as he was he sallied forth to try and find that fatal tomb.

All that afternoon he wandered like an unhappy spirit over the ground. He knew they had gone two miles or more from the town, and that they penetrated a wood. He searched every copse and thicket he could see, but in vain. He found nothing like the scene of their midnight adventure, and returned dispirited in the evening to his hotel. The next day he again sallied out and wandered to and fro in his quest, wearying himself in vain, for he could find nothing like the place he was looking for. A *carabiniere* saw him, and watched his devious movements with suspicion.

"The *Signore* seems to be seeking something," said he.

"I am looking for a tomb," said Bryant.

"The *Signore* should apply to the *custode* who will guide him. All the tombs are closed, and visits are not permitted without the *custode*."

Bryant murmured something in reply, and wandered on while the *carabiniere* kept the eye of suspicion upon him. In the evening he staggered home. No news had come from Chiarina, and in despair, utterly worn out, and broken down, he threw himself on his bed, and gave himself up for lost.

Dr. Morton was sitting in his rooms at Oxford after breakfast, smoking his morning pipe, and casting an eye occasionally at the notes of a lecture he was to give that morning on folk-lore. In writing it he had made use of his experiences in Tuscany during the late holiday. The thought of this brought Bryant back to his recollection, and he drew from his pocket a letter received from him a few days back, which had puzzled him a good deal. It was very short, and consisted of a few broken sentences to which he could not attach much meaning. It said:

"I am being bothered and pestered beyond all endurance in a way that drives me mad. I cannot part with that ring. You do not know what I am suffering. One thing is certain, I must obey Antonietta, and go back."

"But why," thought Morton, "does he bother himself about his ring? Why *should* he part with it, if he does not like to do so, and why does he let people pester him about it? Some dealer or other I expect who wants to buy it. But who's there? Come in," he said in reply to a knock at the door.

The newcomer was one of the Fellows who was a great friend of Bryant and Morton after a few words on general matters asked him if he had heard anything of Bryant lately.

"Well, as you ask me," said Williamson, "I have, and I am uneasy about him. You know he wrote a great deal for the *Picadilly* magazine, and in fact was one of their principle contributors. Well I met Henderson, the editor, at the Athenæum the other day, and he said to me, 'What is the matter with your man, Bryant?'

"'Nothing that I know of,' said I. 'Why do you ask?'

"'I ask,' said he, 'because he sent us an article the other day for the *Picadilly* that he could only have written if he were drunk or mad. It was rambling and illiterate, and of course, useless to us.

But the curious thing was that it dragged in head and shoulders a lot about Etruscan tombs, and a fatal ring, that had nothing whatever to do with the subject.'"

"A ring you say," said Morton. "Now that is curious, for I was just reading when you came in, a letter from him that I received a few days ago, about a ring. I remember he did pick up a ring in an old Etruscan tomb we visited together, and one of those half necromantic women of the place prophesied it would bring him no good. He talks also of going back there. I remember the inn where we stayed, and I have a mind to wire out to find out if he is there."

Morton accordingly telegraphed to the *padrone* of the Stella d'Oro at Corneto to ask whether *Signore* Bryant was there, and he prepaid the answer. The answer did not come till the next day. It said:

"The *Signore* is here. Very ill. Prays for you to come."

Morton was much concerned, for he had a great regard for Bryant. Something was evidently wrong, and the ring seemed to be at the bottom of it. Morton remembered saying to Bryant that he would have done better to leave it behind. His researches in folk-lore had revealed to him the superstitious belief of the peasantry in the old Etruscan mythology, and it had sometimes occurred to him, though he always dismissed the idea as absurd, that they might have some ground for their faith. And now here was Bryant evidently in some mysterious way or other in trouble about hr ring he had picked up. Well, at all events, Morton resolved to go at once in answer to his friend's appeal.

In due time he arrived at the Stella d'Oro, and the *padrone* met him with a serious face. "I am glad you are come, *Signore*," said he. "your poor friend has been raving and calling for you. He keeps crying out about a ring and a tomb, and we cannot tell what he means. The doctor shakes his head, and will not say what he thinks."

Morton was much concerned, and asked for particulars of his illness. The landlord said *Signore* Bryant had been very strange, very unlike what he was when Morton had been there with him; that he spent his days wandering about the country as if in search of something, so that the police had noticed it, and had been inquiring about him, as if they suspected him of some mischief. But that at last he had completely worn himself out, and had now been lying a week in a raging fever and delirium.

"You had better come and see him, *Signore*, though I doubt he will not know you."

They mounted the stairs silently, and stole quietly into the darkened room.

"He is very still now," said the *padrone*, as they approached the bed. "I hope he is sleeping; sleep will do him good."

But as Morton bent over his friend and called him by his name he realised that poor Bryant's troubles were over. He was dead.

Morton was excessively shocked, and quite overcome. Bryant had been his most intimate and congenial friend; he had watched with interest his literary career, which promised great things, and he grieved to think a life that had opened so well should be so prematurely cut short. He sat by his poor friend's bedside in sincere distress.

A message was brought to him a little later that a young woman, a Contadina, was below, and asked for the English gentleman. Morton descended, and found himself face to face with Chiarina, who remembered him at once. She explained that she had come in reply to a letter from the English *Signore*, and would have come sooner had it been possible, but she had been away from home for some days.

"And now, Chiarina," said Morton, "you come too late to see him. The poor *Signore* is no more." Chiarina expressed her regret and sympathy, and asked what the poor *Signore* died of.

"He wore himself out," said Morton, "looking I imagine, for the tomb you showed us that night."

"Oh! *Dio*! Surely he did not venture to go there by himself," said Chiarina. "Is it that which has brought this illness on him?"

"No. I think not. He seems to have failed to find it. But he has been in trouble about a ring. You remember he picked one up in the tomb, and your mother told him it would bring him bad luck. What can you tell me about it?"

"Ah! Now I understand," said Chiarina. "*Signore*, that ring has killed him. Those you know of never forgive. You will remember my mother said 'the hand that took must be the hand to restore.' Till he restored it, he would have no peace, and now it has brought him to his death."

"Now," thought Morton to himself, "I understand his return to Corneto, his wild rambling about the place, and his anxiety to find Antonietta and Chiarina. He wanted, of course, to get them to guide him to the tomb and return the ring."

He stood a little while in thought, and then asking Chiarina to await his return, he went back to the chamber of death, and stood by the dead man's bedside. He took the cold hand in his; on the finger was the fatal ring.

"Humph!" said Morton, "There is no knowing what mischief it may do. Perhaps after all the ring had nothing to do with it, and poor Bryant's sufferings may have been imaginary so far as it was concerned. But anyhow, it seems to have plagued him in life, and I should be sorry to think it plagued him in death. On the whole, I had better draw it oft from his finger, and give it to Chiarina to take it back to the place it came from."

# A Romance of the Picadilly Tube

Old Mr. Markham lay dying in an upper room of a fine mansion in a great London square. The house was plunged in that oppressive stillness which reigns when sickness is there and death is near. Footsteps were stealthy, and voices subdued, and the ticking of the clock was audible in the silent room. By the bedside of the old man was Mr. Harvey, his confidential solicitor and old friend, come to attend the execution of the sick man's last will and testament.

"You are quite resolved then," said Mr. Harvey, to dispose of your property thus? I have drawn the will exactly to your instructions, but as an old friend of you and your sons, you will forgive my putting this question again for the last time."

"Yes," said a feeble voice, "that's what I mean."

"You cut off your elder son, George, with a thousand pounds, and leave all the rest, except some minor legacies, to James. The old will, you remember, left them equal shares."

"Yes, yes," said the old man peevishly. "I have paid George's debts over and over again till I am sick of it, and what I might give him now would only go the way of the rest. He has a little money of his own from his mother, if he hasn't spent it, and he must make that do. James is a careful lad and the estate will fare better in his hands."

"Well, I have no right to say more, though I'm sorry. But of course, you must do what you please with your own." The old man was propped up in his bed, a pen was put into his feeble fingers, a servant was called in as a second witness, the deed was duly signed and attested, and Mr. Harvey took it away with him.

The two sons were waiting in the dining-room. They had finished a late luncheon and were standing by the fire. They knew of Mr. Harvey's visit, and had guessed its purpose, and various thoughts were passing through their minds. George indeed did not trouble himself much about the will. In his careless way, he thought things would be alright, and he need not worry himself about them beforehand. He was concerned for his father, whom he really loved, though he knew how often he had plagued and offended him, almost beyond forgiveness. James, on the contrary, being of a cooler and more calculating temper, could not help wondering what was meant by a new will, and an altered disposition of the property. The estate was a large one, with lands in the country, beside the house in town, and large sums in the funds, and he wondered how his interests would be affected by what was going on upstairs.

The door opened and Mr. Harvey came in to bid them goodbye. He had known them since they were boys, and had a regard for both of them, though in his secret heart he preferred scapegoat George to his more careful brother.

"Well, sir," said George advancing to meet him. "How did you leave my father? I am sorry to say the doctor gives us little hope. Do you think he would like to see me?"

"I doubt it George; you must ask the doctor or the nurse. He is very feeble."

"Was he able to attend the business you came about?" asked James.

Mr. Harvey thought the question rather ill-timed and unfeeling, and answered a little curtly, that there had been no difficulty. He then took leave of them. George accompanied him to the door, and as they were parting, Mr. Harvey putting his hand on his arm said:

"Tell me, George, have you any debts?"

"Not a penny," said he radiantly, "my dear old father paid them all off last week before he fell ill. It was awfully good of him. I know I have behaved badly, and did not deserve it from him."

"Well, George," said Mr. Harvey, "let me give you a hint. There must be no more debts in future. You will have to be careful. I speak seriously for your good. Farewell, and don't forget what I say."

Left to himself, George wondered what was meant by this hint, connected, he supposed, with the new will, if indeed a new will had really been executed, as he and his brother believed. Mr. Harvey's words seemed to convey a friendly warning that things had not been favourably for him upstairs. He had always understood that he and his brother were to share equally in the estate; was this arrangement to be disturbed? That would be awkward, for he had only small means of his own, and his way of living had always been after an opulent fashion.

"Hang it all." He said, "it will be deuced hard on me, if James gets more than his share. After all, I'm the eldest son, and he has no right to cut me out."

Like the two sons of the Patriarch, the two Markhams differed entirely in character and pursuits; but in the modern case, the parental preference had been reversed, for it was the mother who had loved the Esau of the family best, and the father who favoured the Jacob. George Markham was lively and adventurous, a lover of pleasure and selfish and self-indulgent in its pursuit; but he had a kindly and generous vein in his composition which in the view of his friends went far towards compensating his faults.

James was of a cautious and calculating nature, who did everything with deliberation, looking carefully after his own interests, and fencing himself with precautions. He was married, and had children, and a business in the City which was doing well. Since his mother's death, George's influence in the family steadily declined. Esau sank into disfavour and the star of Jacob ascended; till at last, as we have seen, their father resolved that by leaving George free of debt and with a thousand pounds in his pocket, he might wash his hands of further responsibility for him.

In this perturbed state of mind, after parting with Mr. Harvey, George avoided rejoining his brother, and taking his hat, sallied forth to go to his chambers in the Temple. The justification for these chambers was a shallow pretence he made of reading for the Bar, though beyond eating his dinners he did little else to qualify himself for a forensic career. However, it served as a pretext for establishing himself in bachelor's quarters, which was convenient for his way of living, and his father had long given up in despair any inquiry after his legal studies.

It was growing dusk as he descended to a station to the Piccadilly tube. There was the congestion of would-be passengers usual at eventide when offices close and myriads of clerks and servants flock from the centre of London to the outskirts. Trains arrived crammed to suffocation, not a seat vacant, passages choked with strap-holders, and entrance lobby solid with perspiring humanity. When the carriage doors were opened to discharge a few travellers, the mob surged desperately to force an entrance, half of them to be disappointed, and condemned to wait for another train, where there might be more fortunate. George was near one end of the platform where the crowd was a little less compact, though even there he had hardly time to move.

A train was heard approaching and every head was turned in that direction. At that moment a gentleman in front of him dropped something, and stooped to recover it, though the crowd allowed him little room for movement. George saw it at his feet: it was a paper folded lengthways and lay more within his reach than that of the owner. "Let me get it for you, sir," he said, and stooped to pick it up and restore it. The roar of the train sounded close at hand; the crowd pressed on the stooping figures, as they rose together they were pushed violently against one another; the other man was close to the edge of the platform, and to his horror, George saw him lose his balance and fall over the edge. As he fell, George caught sight of his face; it was his old friend, Mr. Harvey. The train was upon him in a moment.

There was a shriek from the crowd, first a recoil and then a rush of agonised spectators; George was swept back to the far side of the platform and stood leaning against the wall, trembling and sick with horror. Officials arrived, the train was moved, and men went down on the line upon their ghastly errand. He could not bear to wait and see the recovery of the body, or witness the frightful details of the accident. Shaking in every limb, he found his way to the exit, half unconsciously; the lift was remote and news of the accident had not reached the attendant when George took his place, and there was no delay.

As he reached the surface, he noticed that he had in his hand the fatal paper which had occasioned the disaster. It was too dark to see the address and he put it in his pocket. It had belonged, he supposed, to his poor friend, and on the morrow he would forward it to the address it bore. It did not matter now, his only aim for the moment was to get to his quarters and try to recover his nerve. He called a cab and drove to the Temple.

Arrived at his rooms, he sank into an armchair and covered his face with his hands. The whole dreadful scene passed before him in imagination; the crush, the collision, the reeling back of his poor friend, the glimpse of his face and of the grey hair as his hat fell off, and then the train came upon him. It made him sick to think of it. By and by, as the first horror of the scene passed and left room for calmer reflection, he thought less of the accident, and more of the man.

Harvey had long been his father's friend and adviser; he had always been kind to himself a s a boy, and had often stood his friend when he had need of an advocate with his father He thought of him with affection, and remembered how many times he had given him sound advice which had never been followed, but of which he now saw the value; and now that was all at an end, and what an end!

After a time he rose, and thought he would go and dine somewhere quietly. He could not bear to go to his club and face his friends with this horror fresh on his mind, and so he had a quiet chop at one of his old eating-houses in Fleet Street, where he knew he should meet no one of his acquaintance, and it was late when he came back to his chambers.

When he had turned on the light, his eye fell upon something that lay on the table. It was the fatal paper, which he had taken from his pocket before going out. He took it up listlessly, to see if it bore any address to which he should send it in the morning. But it bore no address, and when he had read the endorsement, he stood for a few minutes motionless with the paper in his hand, as if he were turned to stone. He saw it was a will, or rather a codicil to the last will and testament of Richard Markham, which had been executed that very afternoon. After a time, he laid the paper again on the table, and stood with his back to the fire thinking what he should do.

So there really had been a new will, or a codicil to alter the old one, had from the hint dropped by his poor friend, Mr. Harvey, he gathered that the alteration had not been in his favour. The temptation was strong to open the paper and see how he stood, but he was restrained by a scruple, and continued to stand by the fire looking at it as it lay on the table before him. He supposed that his loss would be James's gain. James had always been his father's favourite, comparisons had been drawn between him and James, to James's advantage; James had been proposed to him as a pattern though he hated James's cautious ways which seemed to him mere selfishness.

The selfishness of his own idle extravagant life naturally did not occur to him. James, he thought, was a schemer, who had always got the better of him, and had robbed him of his birthright as eldest son. What would be the justice of James taking more than a fair share of his father's estate? The longer he thought about it the stronger grew the temptation to open the paper and see what provision it made for him. There it lay before him, as it were looking him in the face and inviting him to take it; a riddle awaiting a solution, charged with fate and the whole current of his future life. He took it in his hand and weighed it: on this fatal sheet his fortunes depended.

In a matter so vital it was folly to be over-scrupulous; as he gathered he was the person most likely to be affected by its contents; surely he was entitled to know them, and it could not matter to anyone else whether he knew them or not.

He sat down and opened the paper, it was a codicil to the old will, very short, and it dealt almost entirely with the one subject of George's share in the disposition of the estate. He laid the paper down in dismay, and sat in silence looking into the fire.

"A thousand pounds and nothing more," he kept repeating to himself. "It is monstrous. What have I done to deserve to be treated thus?" Independently of the money, how was he to explain his position to the world, for his friends had always looked on him as his father's heir. How was he to live on the slender income inherited from his mother, which luckily for him, she had so tied up that he could not touch the capital? All his habits and tastes were expensive; he constantly outran his father's liberal allowance, and as constantly had to appeal to him for money to clear his debts.

There was no one now left to appeal to, for it would be idle to approach James, who he knew would stand on his rights and give him his thousand pounds and no more? Besides which he could not bring himself to beg of his younger brother; no, that at all events was not to be thought of—and there lay the accursed paper in his lap. What was to be done with it? He supposed it ought to go to Messrs. Harvey & Moor, his father's lawyers. But that might wait till tomorrow. And poor Harvey was dead. That however did not affect the matter, for the firm was there. He must send it to them tomorrow, he supposed.

It was then that some pestilent devil at his elbow seemed to whisper in his ear, "Why send it at all?"

The idea covered him with shame and he scouted it at first, for reckless as his life had been he had never stooped to anything dishonourable. But it would not be so dismissed, and kept pestering him with suggestions of the ease with which the codicil might be suppressed. Putting things together he made out that Mr. Harvey had taken the codicil to Mr. Markham, who had signed it, the witnesses being Mr. Harvey himself and the footman, whose names appeared in the document; that Mr. Harvey had taken the paper away with him, and had arrived at the station on the Piccadilly tube at pretty nearly the same moment when he got there himself. The rest of the story we know.

"Then," thought George, "one of the witnesses was dead, and the footman could only testify that he signed a paper, not knowing what it was, which might have been something quite different." The lawyers, of course had instructions for drawing the codicil, and probably a rough draft of its contents, but what evidence could they produce that it had ever been executed? The only proof of that was the codicil itself and that now lay in his lap; and the fire was burning opposite him.

It would only be an affair of a moment, the hateful deed would be reduced to a few ashes, and he would inherit the half of the estate to which he maintained he was entitled by every consideration of justice and fair-play. James would have the other half, which was his fairly enough, and he was already doing well in business, and so would really be much better off than his elder brother. The temptation was strong; almost irresistible; the devil at his elbow kept urging him; and his very fingers itched to twitch the fatal paper from his lap on to the glowing coals. But his better self restrained him: he could not bring himself to do it, and locking the deed up in his drawer he went to bed.

He was roused next morning by a messenger from his father's house, with a letter from his brother James, enclosing another addressed to himself:

"Dear George," it began, "You will not be surprised to hear that all is over here. Our dear father died quietly last night. You will, no doubt, come at once to help me make the necessary arrangements. I enclose a letter for you from Messrs. Harvey & Moor, which, as it was marked 'immediate', I ventured to open. You will be shocked at its contents. Your affectionate brother, James Markham."

Messrs. Harvey & Moor's letter announced the unfortunate death of the elder partner from an accident on the railway. They thought, as he was engaged in business for Mr. Markham at the time of his decease, they ought to lose no time in communicating the sad intelligence to Mr. Markham's representative.

George had not expected his father's death so suddenly, and was much affected. He wished he had been with him at the end. Their relations had not always been friendly, but he admitted the fault had been his own, though the punishment in the end was unfairly severe, he went home therefore with mixed feelings of sorrow and resentment.

He alighted at the same station on the tube railway which had been the scene of the catastrophe the night before, and he looked with horror at the fatal spot. As he made his way to the lift he had an uncomfortable feeling that he was being followed, to be sure a crowd was going with him, but it was not that; he saw no one especially noticing him, and could not account for the feeling. He had given up his ticket and entered the lift, when the attendant said "Ticket please," to someone behind him. He turned but saw no one.

"Old gentleman with you, sir?" asked the attendant. "Why, what has become of him?" he continued looking about him.

"No. There is no one with me," said George, much surprised.

"Well, I'm dashed," said the attendant, staring about. "He's gone, anyhow. That's rummy"; and then he attended to his duty and started the lift.

George found the great house with all the windows darkened: the straw with which the street had been strewn during the late owner's illness deadened all sound from outside, and within was the silence of death. James met him, already attired in funeral weeds, and his wife was there whom George dislike, for he thought her intriguing and meddlesome, and mistrusted her influence on James himself. He knew instinctively he had no friend in her should any question arise about the disposition of the estate. He went and saw his father; the tears stood in his eyes as he thought of the unkindness that had grown up between them year by year, and he was touched with remorse as he recalled the many occasions on which he had given cause for his father's displeasure.

He even, at that moment, forgave him that fatal codicil, though the feeling of resentment returned as he sat at luncheon with James and his wife, and thought how unfairly they were to benefit at his expense. He took his part in the arrangements for the funeral and other matters, but would not stay in the house, and returned in the evening to his chambers in the Temple, anxious and dispirited, and with a sense of impending calamity. And then he remembered that he was to have sent that paper to the lawyers in the morning, and had not done so. Well, it was too late tonight he would do it in the morning. He would be glad to be rid of it and be put out of his misery.

His sleep was not untroubled. He seemed to go back to the time when he was a boy, and his father a younger man, who had been kind to him and proud of his performances in his school games, at which James had always been a duffer; and then his father's face grew serious and displeased as it had become in later life; and then it melted away into another face, the face of his old friend Harvey, sad and warning, and oh, horror! There were streaks of blood, and with that he awoke. Morning was beginning, he could sleep no more; a cold bath restored his nerves, and a walk in the brisk morning air before breakfast braced him up somewhat for the coming day.

Days passed and the time came for the funeral, and after that he knew the executors would be moving in the matter of the will, and questions would arise about the codicil. It still lay in his drawer. He had put off from day to day taking the irrevocable step of sending it, which would deprive him at once of all claim to what he held was his rightful inheritance. He said to himself it was useless to put it off; it could make no difference to him whether he sent it now, or kept it a few days longer: the result would be the same; and yet he had not the courage to do the fatal act. The pistol was at his head as it were, and his finger on the trigger, and he dared not pull it, though he knew he was doomed. He grew pale and anxious and avoided society.

Of James he saw as little as possible, though family arrangements made it necessary they should meet sometimes. He fancied his sister-in-law looked at him with an air of subdued triumph, though what she could know about the codicil and its contents? It raised his bile and hardened his heart, and he thought how easily if he pleased he could defeat her.

Mr. Markham's executors were, two, Mr. Winter, a City magnate, and Sir Charles Mallet, a retired Indian civilian, and they were already in communication with the solicitor firm of Harvey & Moor. The only will in evidence was that made some years before, which gave the two brothers an equal share in the estate. But Mr. Moor produced the draft of the codicil which upset this arrangement, and which he believed had been duly executed, though at present it could not be found.

"What makes you think it was executed?" asked Sir Charles.

"I think so," said Mr. Moor, "because we had Mr. Markham's instructions to send it to him for signature, he being then ill in bed. It was therefore copied out fairly, and my partner, Mr. Harvey, took it with him to Mr. Markham's house. He was seen there by both the sons, and we know that Mr. Markham signed something, for a servant, whom we can produce, witnessed it, and we presume it was the codicil. Mr. Harvey, as you know, was unhappily killed on his way home, and the document which he no doubt had with him was, we presume, lost or destroyed in the accident."

"What the servant witnessed," said Mr. Winter, "may have been only a transfer of stock or something of that kind."

"Perhaps, but we are not aware of any such transfer being made at that time."

"On the other hand," said Sir Charles, "Mr. Markham may have changed his mind and altered the codicil before signing it. I confess it seems to me it was a monstrous piece of injustice from first to last."

"Well, gentlemen, what do you suggest?" said Mr. Moor.

The executors debated about the matter a little linger and at last it was agreed to have another meeting at which the two

Markham sons, who were principally concerned, should be present.

"What could induce my old friend Markham to make such a change in his will as that unhappy codicil was to have done?" said Sir Charles as the two executors walked away together.

"I know he was much put out by his elder son's extravagance," said the other, "and had paid a deal of money at times to get him out of debt. I suppose he thought that should be brought into the account."

"Well, I should be sorry for if George lost his share. He is a good fellow at bottom," said Sir Charles, "and I dare say he has sown his wild oats by now. But what about this tiresome codicil? Do you think it was really execute, and if so, shall we ever find it?"

"Goodness knows," said Mr. Winter. "At all events I think it will give us a lot of trouble. Dear me! Who would be a trustee or executor?"

"I don't like James, the younger brother," said Sir Charles. "George is a much better fellow, though he has been playing the fool."

"And it is James," said Mr. Winter, "whose interest it is to put forward the codicil."

"You mean he will oppose the probate if we propound the old will without it?"

"Well," said Mr. Winter, "I know something of James in the City, and he is a good man of business."

"I see," said Sir Charles. "Goodbye; here I think our ways part." And then they shook hands and separated.

The proposed meeting at which the two brothers were to attend was fixed about a week later at Mr. Markham's house, where James Markham and his family were staying to see about the necessary domestic arrangements. Thither, at the time appointed, George Markham made his way, alighting at the tube station nearest the house as usual. He hated the sight of the place, which had such painful associations, and had he thought of it, he would have come another way, but from force of habit he had unconsciously followed the usual route. As he gave up his ticket at the lift the attendant looked hard at him, and then beyond him over his shoulder. The man's manner made George turn round to see what he was looking at. But he saw nothing.

"He's gone again," muttered the man. "I don't 'alf like it. Bill," said he to another attendant when he had discharged his living cargo at the top, "did ye see that grey-haired old gen'lman as come to the lift at the bottom, but didn't get in?"

"Not me," said Bill, who was not interested. "Well, but look ye here! He follers that gen'lman as you see there walking away, up to the lift, and when I arst 'im for 'is ticket, why—he isn't there."

"Trying to bilk the company, very likely," said Bill. "If you can ketch 'im. P'rhaps, you'll get a reward."

"Don't be a fool, Bill," said the other. "I tell you this has happened every time that same man comes 'ere. And I'll tell you another thing," said he, lowering his voice. "Do you remember that accident the other day when an old gentleman was killed?"

"Why of course I do. What of that?"

"Why, as they carried 'im away, I see 'is face, and I see that face again just now at the foot of the lift."

"Oh, go along with you!" said Bill, as he walked away. "I don't believe in ghosties—you've been drinking and got the horrors."

The meeting took place in the dining-room. Both the executors were present with Mr. Moor, and George and James, by whose side his wife was sitting, with whom he frequently conferred in a whisper.

Both brothers had, of course, been formally made acquainted by the solicitor with the terms of the will, and also of the missing codicil.

But the solicitor stated the case afresh to make sure that it was understood in all its bearings by those concerned. The old will was obviously to be put forward for probate: about that there was no room for difference of opinion. The only difficulty was about the codicil. The codicil being missing, the question was one of proof that it had ever been executed.

Sir Charles Mallet said the whole thing was very uncertain. Even if the codicil had been duly executed, of which positive evidence seemed wanting, how were they to know whether it had been signed without alteration?

"It is not for me," he continued, "to criticise Mr. Markham's motive in making that codicil, but the effect of it, if I may be allowed to say so, is so unusual in the difference it makes between his sons, and so serious in the case of the elder brother, that it is quite conceivable that the testator may have changed his mind before signing. A stroke of the pen, for instance, might have converted Mr. George Markham's thousand pounds into ten or twenty thousand, or even more."

Mr. Winter, the other executor, seemed to concur with this view. He said he did not quite see his way to act on the draft codicil in the absence of the document itself. But of course, he would be guided by the lawyers.

"I think," began James, "my dear father's last wishes but here he was stopped by marks of disapproval on the faces of his auditors.

"You were about to say something, Mr. Markham," said the solicitor.

Mrs. James had been whispering to her husband, and obedient to her prompting he proceeded.

"I was going to ask whether we should be doing right if we disregarded what we positively know to have been my father's last wishes as to the disposition of his estate."

"You mean that you should take my share as well as your own?" said George, who had not spoken before.

But James took no notice of this remark. "Do I understand," said Mr. Moor, "that you will oppose the probate of the will with the codicil?"

"Well, I am of course in a somewhat difficult position," said James, "being an interested party. But I have to consider others as well as myself, who would be affected; for myself, I might be disposed to waive any claim, but there is my wife, and there are my children, who would have rights in the matter, and so—well, gentleman, you see the difficulty of my position."

His speech ended rather lamely, and it was received by the company in silence. Sir Charles looked at his colleague and raised his eyebrows. The other nodded, and the party broke up without any formal resolution, it being understood that the executors would be guide by legal advice in their procedure.

Sir Charles shook hands with George as they went out, and said it was an awkward business, and he was sorry for him if things went wrong. As for James, Sir Charles managed to avoid his parting salute.

"James showed very badly," he said to his colleague as they walked away. "He should have held his peace. That cant about his wife and children was in bad taste."

"You'll see James means to have his knife into his brother," said Mr. Winter. "We are in for a lawsuit over this business if I am not much mistaken."

Meanwhile the codicil still lay lurking in the drawer of George's writing-table in the Temple. The longer he deferred sending it, the harder it seemed to be to do so. He still said to himself he supposed it had to be done, but the more he thought about it the more cruel did the necessity appear. It was monstrous injustice to rob him of what his father had intended to give him by the will. Sir Charles Mallet had almost said as much at the meeting, and when he shook hands with him at parting. And James, with his hypocritical pretence of shielding himself behind the absurd rights of his wife and children!

If anything would make him keep back the codicil it would be a desire to defeat James and his odious wife. James, with half the estate and a flourishing business in the City, was a rich man already, richer than he himself would be, even if he got his share. James ought to be satisfied with that, and not try to rob his elder brother of his rightful inheritance. With these thoughts George worked himself up into a passion of resentment against his brother, his sister-in-law, the codicil, the lawyers who drew it, and everyone concerned about it, and persuaded himself that he was the injured victim of a conspiracy to defraud and beggar him. And all the while the same pestilent little devil at his elbow kept whispering, "Don't send it, don't send it; burn it, burn it."

And yet, when he got to his chambers, took it out of the drawer, and looked at it and at the fire, he could not do it.

"Not yet, not yet," he said to himself, and he put it back into the drawer and locked it up. But he had taken a step nearer the fatal act, and the next step would be a short one.

And James; he too was not quite happy. He had been greatly surprised to learn the contents of the codicil, which went far beyond any change he had imagined it would make in the disposition of the estate. He was not without affection for his brother, who had protected him at school, though he laughed at him and thought him a muff, and who had always acted generously to him as they grew up. Underneath a crust of cols selfishness still glowed the embers of their old friendship, and his first thought on reading the lawyer's communication had been: "It is very hard on poor George; what will he do?" it even occurred to him to let the matter of the codicil drop, especially as the document itself had been lost, and there was no positive proof of it ever having been executed.

He was well off; the estate was a large one, and half of it with what he had would make him a rich man. He could afford to let George's half go as the old will had intended it should. But, unhappily, James consulted his wife, who over-persuaded him, and suggested the arguments which he had employed at the meeting, and by which, with her help, he at last succeeded in convincing himself. His father no doubt thought he was acting for the best, and his last wishes ought to be sacred; he had never cost his father a penny since he started in life, whereas George had bled his father's purse freely over and over again, and that surely ought to be taken into account.

And then there were his wife and children—but here he paused: the faces of the executors at the meeting when he used that argument recurred to his memory, and he felt it would not do. He even blushed slightly at the recollection, and felt he had lowered himself by stooping to such a shallow pretence, which deceived nobody, not even himself.

Had James at this point been left alone he was not incapable of a generous decision. He had half a mind as he left the meeting and realised the unfavourable impression his claims had made on the executors, to write to the lawyer and say he waived any claims he might have arising from the codicil, and was content to abide by the original will; but he reckoned without his wife. Her tears and reproaches overcame his weak leaning to the generous side, and he resolved to claim his legal rights under the missing codicil, if his lawyers advised him that he had a good case.

The matter therefore had to be decided in a court of law, for the executors decided on ignoring the draft codicil, and propounded the original will. There was a special jury empanelled, and the highest talent of the Bar was employed on either side. James and his wife were there throughout the whole proceedings. George would not go near the place. In a manner he was relieved by the course things were taking. If the court decided that the codicil was to be upheld, why he had done no harm by keeping it hidden; the result would only be the same as if it had never been lost.

If, on the other hand, the codicil should be negative, he would take it as his justification in suppressing what he held to be an unfair invasion of his rights as the elder son. He was not really satisfied with these arguments; his conscience told him he was guilty of a dishonest act, and so far prevailed that he could not bring himself to show his face in court. He therefore spent the day in the country; the trial, he was told, would certainly take all day, and he would hear the result when he returned in the evening.

He had a long tramp over the Surrey hills, from Epsom racecourse to Headley Common and Boxhill, returning by Mickleham and Leatherhead. The day was lovely, the larks singing in a sky of heavenly blue, the tees were still decked in the fresh virgin green of spring, and there was that delicious brisk buoyancy in the air that makes a man say life is worth living. But to George, at that time, it did not seem so. Life seemed to him a sordid affair. Take his own case; think of the choice before him: on one hand to be honest and a beggar, or on the other to be wealthy and a thief.

Was such a life worth living in either case? Between the horns of this dilemma he was miserable. It haunted him as he walked, and he ate his solitary luncheon at the wayside inn. His conscience troubled him; his honour in any case was smirched; whatever reparation he might make would not wipe off the stain; and that being so, that pestilent little tempter suggested, "Why worry about it? You have gone so far, you can't undo the fact that you have been guilty; it is too late to mend matters; go home and burn the deed. If the jury decide against you it won't be wanted, and if they decide for you it will be best in the fire to make things safe."

It was with this resolution finally fixed in his mind that George returned to town and sought his chambers. A telegram and some notes lay on his table, as he naturally supposed containing a report of the result of the trial. He felt no impatience to learn what it was; he was disgusted with himself and the whole business.

The telegram was from the lawyers, and said:

"Will maintained, codicil upset."

A later note from them confirmed this, and offered congratulations. Another note from Sir Charles Mallet, warmly expressed, said how glad he was of the result: that for his part he could not believe his old friend Mr. Markham really had signed a deed which was so obviously unjust.

"If he only knew," said George to himself, "that the codicil lies at this moment in the drawer under my hand, what would he think of me?"

He sat down to consider what he should do. He was now a rich man, but he felt no elation. It was however impossible to draw back. He must go on to the end. If ever the codicil were to be given up, it should have been done before the trial. The half of the estate was now legally his; to give it up would be quixotic. He half persuaded himself that his father, had he lived, would have reconsidered such an unfair division of the estate, and that the result of the trial, could he know it where he was, would not be displeasing to him.

He went to dine quietly at a City eating-house, not feeling fit for society, and unable to face the congratulations of his friends if he went to his club. He sat an hour over his port wine, making up his mind. He now had what he held to be his just rights, and it was necessary to make them secure. If he had made a bargain with the devil, at least he would have the fruits of it. The codicil should be destroyed that night, and James, with his odious wife, should be finally defeated for good and all.

Having made up his mind he went back to his chambers. His mind was in a strange confusion, a sort of nervous oppression weighed on him as he opened the door and entered. A fire was burning in the grate sending flickering gleams about the room. He turned on the lights; unlocked the drawer, and laid the fatal paper on the table. He stood a minute looking at it, and then he suddenly discovered he was not alone. Seated by the fire with his back to him was a man, whose grey head was visible over the top of the easy chair. George was on the point of asking who he was and what he wanted, when something seemed to arrest his speech, and he could only regard his strange visitor in silence.

The figure rose slowly and turned to confront him across the table. The face was the face he had seen in his dream, the face of his old friend Harvey, and it regarded him with an earnestness that penetrated his very soul. George was unable to speak, to act, or even to move. He seemed fixed in a trance and could only look piteously at that serous face and wait in terror for what was to come. Still keeping its gaze fixed on him, the figure advanced to the table and laid its hand on the paper that lay there. Its regard was severe, but not unkindly; it seemed even to express pity and sorrow.

Resting its hand on that fatal codicil it seemed to ask a

question. George knew what it was, and the answer it wanted. Fierce debate raged within him, greed and passion on one side, shame and remorse on the other fought for supremacy, and still that steady gaze penetrated his inmost being. Gradually his evil passions seemed to melt before those calm searching eyes; his conscience awoke to better things; the resolution to do right prevailed. He knew the question that was put to him and in a passion of tears he stammered out, "I will," and sinking into a chair he covered his face with his hands. When he removed them he was alone.

When he recovered himself he rose with a lightened heart, for a weight seemed to have been lifted from him. Reparation, that was the question that he had answered; reparation was what he had promised. It could not be made too soon. It should be made that very night. He put the codicil into an envelope and sealed it and addressed it to Messrs. Harvey & Moor. They need not know whence it came, and so his shame need not be exposed. And yet without confession the reparation would not be complete. He would write to James and tell him all. And in order that James should learn it first from him, and not officially from the lawyers, he would take the letter himself and put it in the letterbox after posting that for the lawyers.

As he walked through the streets in the cool night air he felt happier than he had ever felt in his life. He had done right at last, and had been mercifully saved from consummating his shameful offence. He now looked back on it with horror. What had possessed him to act as he had done? Thank God! He had been spared the worst. His heart was light and joyful, and he could even smile to think of the lawyers' surprise next morning.

He posted his letter and then walked on to his old home, and having dropped the letter for James in the letterbox. Found his way to the tube station, which had been the scene of poor Harvey's accident. Had he really seen his old friend that night, or was it vision of his imagination? He could not tell; whichever it was, it was Harvey who had been his saviour; to Harvey he owed the recovery of his self-respect, the victory over his worse sell. He thought of his old friend with love and gratitude, and thanked God for him.

The platform was congested with people from the theatres which had just closed. Never had he seen such a crowd. The train came up and George was carried in the rush to the entrance of the car. It was over full already; his foot was on the step when the gate was slammed in his face; he could not extricate himself from the crowd; the train began to move, his foot slipped, and was caught between the car and the platform; the train went faster and faster; he was dragged down and down, and he knew no more.

Two missives were put into James Markham's hand early next morning. One was George's letter:

> Dear James,
> I have had the codicil all the time. It came into my hands by a mere accident, and at first I did not even know what was. Tonight I intended to destroy it, but I was prevented by my good angel I have just posted it to Messrs. Harvey & Moor. They will not know whom it comes from. I ask you to keep my secret, to forgive me, and if you can to think kindly of your brother.
>
> George

The other letter was from St. George's Hospital to say that a gentleman, named Markham, had been brought there with injuries received in a railway accident, which it was feared would be fatal, and that he wished to see his brother, Mr. James Markham, before he died.

James was shocked and deeply affected. The old fraternal affection, which had been buried under a load of selfishness and greed, woke within him. George's noble renunciation of the advantage he had won, and candid confession of the wrong he had done, filled him with admiration. He could not help asking himself how he would have behaved had he been subjected to such a trial.

When he stood by George's bedside it was too late. He had

died during the night. The tears stood in James Markham's eyes as he took the cold hand in his, and bending over his brother whispered, "George, I forgive you; your secret is safe with me."

# The Eve of St. John

"He was sitting in his library . . ."

Simple words, which, if one comes upon them in the course of a story call up a pleasing picture of cultured ease, and a literary leisure. One may lay down the book on one's knee, and shut one's eyes, and see in a vision the snug room, crimson-curtained; hear the gentle patter on the hearth of the ashes from the glowing fire, the only sound that breaks the silence, save perhaps the rustle of the leaves, as the occupant turns his page.

On the walls, dimly seen by the light of the shaded lamp, are the well-stored shelves, volumes rich with the sombre splendour of morocco and gilding, folios in the wider shelves below, quartos and octavos above; the spacious leather covered table, with silver inkstand and ample room for atlas volumes, is drawn in front of the master's favourite easy chair, luxuriously padded, leather-clad, and well worn by constant use; before the shining brass fender lies the bearskin rug, beloved by Tim, the fox-terrier, sole sharer with his lord of this temple of study, and comfort, and not infrequently of repose.

It was summer, and the hearth was cold, but otherwise the library in which Cecil Maynard was sitting fully satisfied the conditions of this imaginary picture. It was a lofty and stately apartment with long windows and deep window seats, the fretted plaster ceiling, rich with interlacing ribs and floriated borders bore the arms of the Maynard who had restored and improved the old building three hundred years before, altering it from *château fort* of the middle ages into a habitation suitable to times when private wars had been suppressed, and a better administration of public justice had taken their place.

Through the open casements came the soft summer air bringing in the scent of the hayfield, and in the gathering twilight could just be distinguished well-wooded slopes and green pastures falling rapidly to the river that brawled along its rocky bed, with many an eddy and stickle where the fisherman might look to tempt with his fly a lusty trout.

Cecil Maynard had only a short time before come into possession of the estate of Castle Maynard, which he inherited from an uncle who had died a widower and childless. He knew nothing of the history of his new home, and since taking possession, and settling down after troublesome technicalities of succession, he had amused himself by hunting up information about it in county histories, and by diving into the materials afforded in plenty by family papers in the muniment-room, which had been well kept in orderly arrangement by his predecessors.

He had read of Maynard's who went to the crusades, selling half their estates to raise a contingent of their followers, and impoverishing their successors for several generations. He read of other Maynards who partly retrieved the family fortune only to lose it again in the Wars of the Roses. Recovering their estates under the Tudors, on whose side by a happy accident they had been engaged, they managed to struggle through the civil wars of Charles and the Parliament without much loss of goods, but some loss of credit, owing to the shifty policy of Sir Everard Maynard who then owned the estate, and who by crafty intrigue, and by judiciously trimming his sails to catch the breeze of prosperity that blew sometimes from one quarter and sometimes from another, managed never to compromise himself with the losing part and to turn up in the nick of time on the side of the winner.

At the moment when we are introduced to his successor, sitting in his library that summer evening, he was in fact reading in the county history the story of his ingenious ancestor, of whom he felt he had no particular reason to be proud. As he read on he began to think that political insincerity was not the worst fault that could be laid to Sir Everard's charge, and that there were passages in his life which bore a dubious, not to say, a sinister character. Sir Everard lived to be an old man, and prospered exceedingly, leaving his estates in a more flourishing condition than they had been for a long while before. He died childless, and the estate passed to a distant kinsman.

"Well," said Cecil Maynard, as he closed the weighty folio of his county history, "I am glad at all events that the kinsman from whom I come was only a distant relative; for the less we and ours have of Sir Everard's blood in our veins the better."

The door opened as he spoke, and his young wife came into the room. Mr. Maynard was a year or two younger than her husband. They had only been married a short time before they came to Castle Maynard, and she knew even less about the place than he did.

"Why, Cecil, whatever did you find to pore over in that dusty old volume," said she as she seated herself on the elbow of his chair, and put an arm over his shoulder.

"To tell the truth," said he, "I have been reading the life of a very disreputable ancestor of mine. What is told of him for certain is bad enough, but I doubt whether there is not worse behind. There are many hints given of foul play that never came to light."

"A family romance," said she; "how interesting! How are we to find out more about this disreputable ancestor? I confess he interests me more than all the respectable ones. How long ago did he live?"

"Ah! You women," said Cecil, laughing, "you all of you, I believe, love the sinner rather than the saint."

"Now that's too bad of you," said she, as she kissed the top of his head, the spot which from her position was most accessible to caresses. "I don't love him at all, but I should love to find out what he did. Do go on, and learn more about him. I should dearly like to find that Castle Maynard was the scene of a real tragedy like Dunsinane, or the mystery of Udolpho, or the Castle of Otranto. As it is I have been bitterly disappointed that nobody has ever heard of a ghost in the house. It is hardly respectable in an old family without one."

"A defect no doubt," said Cecil, "of which we ought to be ashamed, and I don't know how we are to make it good. But listen, Alice, to what *Baker's Chronicle* tells of our disreputable ancestor. I won't bother you with all his political tricks and dishonest manoeuvres to keep in with the winning side. They are bad enough. But listen to this:

> "'This Sir Everard was much respected during his life on account of his prosperity, and the favour in which he was held by the Court. He much increased the family estates, which had sunk to a low condition. He married twice, but left no issue by either marriage. His first wife was an heiress who died suddenly, and her inheritance passed to Sir Everard under a will executed shortly before her death. None of her family benefited thereby, though she had always professed attachment to them. His second wife was the daughter of Sir James Tiptoft, knight and Baronet of that same, and was very beautiful. Sir Everard and his wife did not agree, and it is said she threatened to leave him and bestow her lands on another. Certain it is that she disappeared and was never again heard of. Sir Everard seized on her inheritance, and as the lady's family had sided with Parliament in the late wicked rebellion which ended in the murder of that most Blessed Martyr, King Charles I, Sir Everard was confirmed in possession after the happy restoration of his Sacred Majesty King Charles II. Sir Everard lived to a good old age in much honour, and lies under a handsome monument with his effigy in alabaster in the parish church.'"

"How horrible," exclaimed Alice, "what a monster! Both his wives!"

"You think he murdered them?" said Cecil.

"Why Cecil, of course he did! He was another Bluebeard.

No doubt he poisoned the first and made away with the second. It is as plain as a pikestaff, and why couldn't that stupid musty old Chronicler say so outright instead of going twaddling on about his Blessed Martyr and his Sacred Majesty, as if they had anything to do with it."

"On the other hand," said Cecil, "the first wife *may* have died a natural death. People do so. And the next *may* have run away from her disagreeable husband, and lived happily ever afterwards."

"I don't believe it, Cecil," said she, "and I am sure you don't believe it either."

"Well," said he, "I confess there is not much to be said for Sir Everard's morals. But murder! No! That is a different thing altogether from politics, and I think even Sir Everard might have stuck at that. But what I don't like is to think we enjoy his ill-gotten wealth, whether your view should be the true one or not. It is a disagreeable reflection."

"But it's not our fault," said Alice' "how can we help it? Whom could we give it back to?"

"To be sure," said Cecil, "there's Henry Tiptoft living not ten miles off; but I doubt whether he would make any claim after a couple of centuries. And by the way, I remember now hearing of another shady ancestor who lost most of his fortune in play with Sandwich and Dashwood, and Wilkes, and the Dilettanti lot, so let us hope Sir Everard's money went that way. Our present wealth comes from my great grandfather, the famous admiral, and that at all events is clean money, honestly earned in fighting the French."

"Let us get a candle and go and look at Sir Everard's portrait in the picture gallery," said she. "I shall regard him in future with increased interest, for a mystery attaches to him. I wonder what became of that poor second wife. I shall never rest till I find out."

Arm linked in arm they mounted the grand staircase and reached a long gallery at the top of the house where pictures of deceased Maynards hung in a long series, some by famous artists, some by indifferent hands of little merit. Sir Everard's picture was among the best works of Sir Peter Lely, who, though he generally devoted his art to what Walpole calls "the Court of Paphos," occasionally painted a man, in a style both graceful and masculine. The countenance riveted their attention. It was handsome and refined, and at first sight attractive; but the longer you looked at it the less you liked it. Behind its superficial beauty there seemed to be a certain craftiness, a slyness in the eye, a satirical curl in the mouth. The figure was draped in a rich coat of crimson velvet, with ruffles and lace cravat, and in the background was a rough perfunctory likeness of Castle Maynard.

"Well," said Cecil, "what do you think of him?"

"I think," said she, "he looks like a cruel man, and I could believe anything of him."

"Poor Sir Everard," said Cecil. "He won't get any favours from you. But it is very late and time we went to bed. So say goodbye to him and let us go."

Cecil resolved to search among the family papers on the morrow for more information about this uncomfortable member of his family; and it was agreed that they should go to the church and have a good look at the alabaster effigy which preserved the likeness of that shifty politician.

The Church of Castle Maynard stood a little way from the house just outside the park gate and at the end of the village street. Long and low its walls of flint and stone, hoary with age, embosomed amid immemorial yews and shady elms, it was a typical example of an English village church. There are no such village churches in other countries as those of rural England; modest and yet comely, simple and yet refined, gems of homely art and beautiful restraint, rich in interest both historical and artistic, no two of them really alike, and each, unless it has been spoilt by later bad taste, generally possessing some charm that distinguishes it from any other.

Cecil's ancestors were buried in an aisle or chapel belonging to the family. There were brasses inlaid in the floor with inscriptions in black letter; tablets on the walls, of more recent date, recording merits and virtues not perhaps remarkable during life, but discovered after the death of the persons whom they commemorated; altar tombs with recumbent effigies, and knightly armour hanging above; and lastly Sir Everard's monument, the most sumptuous of them all, a Jacobean structure of marble, black, red, and white, against the wall, where under an arch Sir Everard in alabaster, painted and gilt, lay on his side raising himself on one elbow, and with a dog at his feet.

A fulsome epitaph recorded his virtues with an unblushing assurance that made one think Sir Everard must have written it himself to forestall what his successor might perhaps say of him; and indeed it was said that the tomb was constructed in his lifetime, which accounted for its being in an earlier style than the date of his death warranted.

The morning sun was shining brightly through the window traceries, and flickering lights and shadows played over wall and monument, as the wind gently tossed the boughs of the trees and the trailing sprays of ivy that clung to the wall outside, when Cecil and his wife stood before the monument of the redoubtable Sir Everard. The old sexton and verger was within them listening as Cecil translated the cumbrous Latin for the benefit of his wife.

"Law, sir," said he, "do'ee reelly say arl that 'bout Sir Everard? I alms her tell as he was a bad 'un, beggin' your parding, sir, you bein' a relation."

"Yes, Walter," said Cecil, "it does say all that. Whatever he may have been in life, you see that is what he would like us to think of him after he was gone."

"Then Mr. Maynard, sir, I suppose many of these 'ere writings is no better than so many lies?"

"So it is, I fear," said Cecil. "But tell me, is there any monument to either of Sir Everard's wives? I know he was married twice."

"The first wife, sir, lies buried among her own people at Chaldicote? They took her away. I've heerd tell, to spite Sir Everard."

"And the second wife, where does she lie?"

Old Walter looked uncomfortable, and shifted from one leg to the other and scratched his head before replying.

"That I can't tell 'ee, sir," said he. "They do say, but—well—I don't know nothing about it."

"But what do they say, Walter?" said Mrs. Maynard. "I am interested in that poor lady, and want to know all about her."

"Well, mum, when Squire arst me where she lie, I says I don't know. No more I don't, and wot's more, no more don't anybody know. But they do say," and here old Walter lowered his voice, "they do say she don't lie nowhere, and that she walks."

"And have you seen her, Walter?"

"No, no, mum, I never see her," he replied hastily. "Oh no! I never see her. But beggin' your parding, it's time for me to ring the bell and I must go. Oh, no! I never see 'er."

And so saying the old man shuffled off, as if to avoid any more questions on the subject.

"So you see, Cecil," said his wife, "we have a ghost in the family after all. Isn't it delicious?"

He laughed, and led her out into the sunshine. They wandered a little among the tombs reading an inscription here and there. Many of the gravestones went back to the seventeenth century, and if the dead who lie here could speak," said they, "we might learn a good deal about Sir Everard, for they must have known him."

"But look there," said Alice, pointing to a headstone covered with hoary lichen that almost obliterated the inscription, "is not that word, Everard?"

"So it is, said Cecil, and he stooped down to read the epitaph. With some trouble he made it out as follows:

*Here lyeth*
*Roger Trumball Gent.*
*Sometime Steward to the*
*Noble Knight Sir Everard*
*Maynard. June 24 1662*
*There is no device in the*

Here is one, at all events, who knew him well," said Cecil, "but what a strange text to put on a man's grave! One would think it was chosen by someone who owed him a grudge, and was glad to get him buried."

"Sir Everard again no doubt," said Mrs. Maynard, "the words, 'the noble knight,' betray him. It is just his style."

"Poor Sir Everard," said Cecil, "you believe he murdered his two wives, and now I suppose you will have it that he murdered his steward, Roger Trumball, gent., and put up the tombstone to show his malice."

"Well, I shouldn't wonder if it were so," said she.

Cecil burst out laughing, and said though Sir Everard was a trimmer and time-server, and a grabber of inheritances, it was going a long way further to make him a three-folk murderer as well, and so they both laughed and strolled back towards the castle.

"I fancy we are getting Sir Everard on the brain," said Cecil as they wandered slowly over the pleasant green-sward. "Let us not forget all about him; he is really not worth remembering, for though he may not be the bloodstained villain you would make him out, he was a mean trickster, and an unscrupulous and treacherous politician. Let us leave him there."

"Why no, my dear," said she, "I wonder by the way, whether the Tiptofts could tell you anything about her. Henry Tiptoft is an old college friend of mine. We were at Merton together. Suppose we ask him to come and stay a day or two. He can bring his fly-rod and try for a trout, and there are lots of rabbits on the hill that want shooting."

The invitation was sent and accepted for the following week. Sir Henry Tiptoft, of Tiptoft Manor, baronet and justice of the Peace, was the Maynard's nearest neighbour and a young man a couple of years Cecil's senior, though they had been at Oxford together for more than a year. Any difference between the families arising from the unhappy marriage of the heiress of one branch of the Tiptofts with Sir Everard, and her mysterious fate, had long been forgotten and the Maynards and Tiptofts had for some generations been intimate friends.

But as Cecil stood in his library with Henry Tiptoft's letter in his hand, and the memory of their morning walk and visit to the church fresh in his mind, he could not help recalling the ugly story of his crafty ancestor's marriage with poor Hilda Tiptoft, and of its mysterious sequel. From old Walter's hints he gathered that it had passed into the legendary stage among the villagers, and that a superstitious fear prevented their talking of it. But it all happened nearly three hundred years ago, and what thought he, could they know about it?

The truth must have come out long since, had there been anything in the story more than ordinary parting of an uncongenial couple. And if she was never heard of again it might only be that she hid herself, so that her husband should never find her. And yet it was a queer story.

"Her disappearance," said Cecil to himself, "seems to have caused some excitement at the time Sir Everard's successors must have troubled themselves a good deal about it. I wonder whether there is anything among the papers in the muniment-room to throw any light upon it. I'll go and have a hunt."

The muniment-room was a small chamber in an angle turret secured with iron bars. Within, the deeds and parchments were arranged on shelves in tin boxes carefully labelled; and in pigeon holes and drawers, numbered and dated, were papers of all kinds, old letters, old accounts, various documents of more or less interest bearing on the family history. Cecil was by this time becoming pretty well acquainted with the collection, and readily put his hand on the papers relating to the latter part of the seventeenth century.

There were farming accounts, notes of lawsuits in which Sir Everard apparently dabbled a good deal, for he seemed to have disagreed with most of his neighbours. There were letters, some of them written by him to his parents when a little boy at Westminster, full of innocent, schoolboy prattle, and generally ending with a petition for money. Dr. Busby, that great man who had flogged sir Roger de Coverley's grandfather, figured in them sometimes as an awful being, too great to be criticised. It was pathetic, in view of the writer's after career, to read these simple childish epistles full of happy, youthful spirits and warm home affections. Cecil put them back with something like a sigh. Among the letters was a lock of fair curly hair tied with a faded blue ribbon, and wrapped in a paper on which was written in a woman's hand:

"my dear boy's hair on his first going away to school."

"It would have been better for poor Sir Everard," thought Cecil, "had he died young, an innocent warm-hearted school-boy."

As he replaced the parcel of letters, he dislodged from a corner where it seemed to have been purposely concealed with some care, a small packet of papers in a sealed wrapper, endorsed in a clerkly hand on the outside. "Roger Trumball, 1662."

"Oh!" said Cecil to himself, "Roger Trumball! That is the man whose tombstone had that text from Ecclesiastes upon it. If I remember, he is described as Sir Everard's steward. I dare say these are only bills, or accounts of rents, or sales of stock, of no particular interest." He was just going to put the parcel back where he found it, but on second thoughts he broke the seal and glanced at the contents. Something that caught his eye made him pause, and after a moment's reflection he locked up the muniment-room and took Roger Trumball's packet with him back to the library.

The packet consisted only of about a dozen loose sheets of paper, written evidently at different times, and in a hand sometimes beautifully clear in the fine calligraphy of that age, and sometimes merely scribbled as if in haste or fear. On the inside of the wrapper were these words:

I, Roger Trumball, being in deadly fear for my lyfe, put these papers where perchance they will be found and ye truth known. Lord, how long shall ye wicked, how long shall ye wicked triumph.

This portends something serious, thought Cecil, as he drew his chair to the table, and spread the manuscripts before him. They were all dated, and he arranged and read them in order. The first one was imperfect, beginning in the middle of a sentence,

.....comying home of my ladye. Would God things were better ordered for her. I cannot but grieve.

The next paper was dated 1661, and seemed to be written after an interval.

Sept. 15, 1661—Strange things have happened today. My duty calls me to continue this record for my dear ladye's sake. Today my master called me to the small parlour. There was a table set and my Ladye Hilda sat thereat, with a parchment before her and pen and ink. She looked pale, poore sowle. My master was walking up and downe the room seemlinglie much distraught. 'now Hilda,' he said speaking as it were mildly. 'here is Roger come to witness your signature.'

'Roger,' he said to me, 'you will sign here as witness after my ladye.' But my ladye made no movement and sat with her pretty hands in her lap.

'Come Hilda,' said he, 'we are waiting, what is wrong with you?'

'I will not sign this,' said she at last speaking low.

'What,' said he in his softest manner, 'and why not, my dear?'

My ladye cast on him a look of contempt, mistrusting his gentleness. 'You know why,' at last she said, 'you know my condition.'

'What, and let half your land go to your beggerly Round-head Tiptoft cousins! By heaven! No!' said he.

'The land is mine,' said my ladye, 'and I love my cousins.'

My cousin stamped on the floor. The evil look I know so

well came into his face.

'By God!' he said furiously. 'sign it you shall; alive or dead, I'll have all the land from you.;

'You will never get it by frightening me,' said my dear ladye, who has a fine bold way with her when she is miss-poken. My master in a passion snatched ye parchment up. 'Go,' said he to me, and I left the room much concerned for my poor ladye, and doubting some mischance."

There was an interval of nearly two months between this paper and the following one, which was written less carefully.

*Nov. 5. 1661.*—truly I am grieved to the heart for my poor ladye. My master treateth her unkindly, for though he speak softly, his tongue deviseth mischiefs like a sharp razor, working deceitfully, as saith the Psalmist. This day I had occasion to speak with him on the matter of Bullfinch Acre, and I found him on the terrace with my ladye. As I came near I heard him say: 'To give your lands to those Tiptofts is but a kind of treason. They are Roundheads and enemies to the throne now so happily restored.'

'And so were you a Roundhead as you call them,' said my ladye, 'when Oliver ruled the roost. At all events my poor cousins have not ratted from a falling house.'

'Oh, my dear,' said he, 'I now know better. I have learned on which side the right lies.'

'I think,' said my ladye firing up, 'you are a better judge upon which side the might lies.' This roused my master's choler, and turning on his heel, he saw me.

'What, eavesdropping, Roger? I have a good mind—' said he, raising his cane as if to strike me. But I looked him in the face and he saw I was not one to take a beating quietly. 'What brings you here listening to what concerns you not?'

I told him my business, and he said I was to take it to him on the morrow, and I left them. Truly, my dear ladye hath a high spirit, and can give a shrewd answer, but what says the Proverb: *A soft answer turneth away wrath, but grievous words stir up anger.*"

*Nov. 12*—My master being away in London on some affairs, and my ladye biding at home alone, she sent the maid Madelon who waiteth on her, to say that she would fain speak with me. This girl is not to my liking, for things are told of her and my master that are not seemly. So she said smirking, and looking out of the corner of her eyes as is her way with mankind:

'Master Roger, my ladye will have you to meet her on the terrace anon.'

'Well, Madelon,' said I, 'I will do my ladye's bidding at once,' and I turned to go, for I liked not her company.

'But why so hasty, Master Roger?' said she playing with her ribbons, 'May we not have a pleasant word together? We have not met for a long while. And what do you think my ladye wants you for?'

'Nay, I know not,' said I, 'she will tell me herself and then I shall know.'

She looked for a minute or so for a further answer, and as none came, she said:

'Well then go for a churl as you are. I am sorry I wasted my words on you,' and so she went. She is a comely lass enough, but a bold one, and I mistrust her. Doth not the wise man say *As a jewel of gold in a swine's snout, so is a fair woman which is without discretion?*'

I found my dear ladye walking alone on the terrace. She was pale and the tears were in her eyes.

'Roger, come here,' said she, 'I want a word with you. I think you are true and that I may trust you.'

'Indeed you may, madam. I would serve you to the death,' said I, for I was sorely grieved to see how sad she was.

'I believe you,' said she, 'and I will tell you what you can do for me. You have seen and heard enough, Roger, to know how things go with me.'

'Alack! Madam,' I said, 'and sore grieved I am that matters

should be so between you and my master.'

'You know, Roger, my people have fought on the losing side, and now they will be made to suffer for it, and I dare say are already in danger.'

'Aye, madam, Sir Charles Tiptoft and your cousins fought for the good cause—I mean for Parliament,' said I correcting myself, for times are changed, and it is not prudent to speak well of the Commonwealth.

'yet you were right, Roger, to call it the good cause, for so I hold it myself. And now my uncle and cousins will be in trouble and lose their lands, if not their lives, and I want to save half of my estate to bestow on them in their need when it will be safe to do so. But Sir Everard prevents me and will have it all.'

I told her that was what I understood from what I had witnessed; and further that I had heard the sequesters were already at Tiptoft Manor taking a valuation of the estate.

'I know nothing of it, Roger, and what I want you to do is to ride over and find out what has happened, and bring me word. They keep everything from me. My own waiting-maid, I believe is a spy upon me, for everything I do or say is reported to Sir Everard.'

I told her on no account to trust Madelon, who I was sure would betray and ruin her if she could. My mistress was much startled at this, and thanked me for my warning. I promised to ride over to Tiptoft which is about ten or twelve miles away, the next morning, and so left her—"

*Nov. 14*, 1661.—This morning, my master still being away, my ladye sent for me to meet her as before on the terrace. I had been to Tiptoft Manor, and I knew she was expecting me. As I appeared, she came anxiously to meet me, and asked what news I brought.

'Alas! Madam,' said I, 'I would I had better news for you, for I bring sad tidings. The Manor is in the hands of the sequesters, and your uncle and cousins are not there.'

I did not tell her that her uncle was in jail, as a supporter of the late Rebellion, and that her cousins were in London trying to get together interest among their friends to save his life, and also, if possible, his estate. She told me she was now at a loss what to do. That she hoped, if her family had been there to have escaped to them, for that her life here was not to be borne any longer. That she had hoped for my help, and that she was so watched and guarded that without aid, her escape was impossible.

'But now,' said she, 'that hope is gone, and I am a wretched woman. I sometimes think he wishes me dead, and then he would have his way with my estate, for my uncle and cousins are in no case to resist him. There is nowhere for me to fly to. But promise me one thing, Roger,' said she.

I said I would faithfully promise to do all she asked me, even at the peril of my life if needs be.

'Then promise me, Roger,' she said, 'that if anything should befall me, you will seek out my cousins and tell them all you know.'

'And what but good should befall such a virtuous and obedient wife?' said a gentle voice behind us, and there stood my master with his evil smile that means mischief. He had come in time to hear my ladye's last words. I trust he did not hear what passed between us before.

'I see, Madam,' he continued, 'you have chosen a confidant, and that you are enlisting my servant against me.'

'You leave me no choice,' she said, 'when do you ever let me see a friend.'

'That you may enlist him also I suppose,' said he, 'No, Hilda, I cannot have another enemy within my borders,' and then, turning sharply to me, 'and you, Master Steward, must be taught to know your place, and not to meddle with what concerns you not.'

I had it in my mind to answer him, yet it might have made matters worse. For what saith the Psalmist?: *I will keep my mouth with a bridle while the wicked is before me.* He gave me an ugly look, and led my poor ladye away into ye house. I much fear evil is intended against her, and what can I do to help her, poor sowle?

"Well, upon my word," said Cecil to himself, laying down Roger's manuscript, and leaning back in his chair when he had read thus far. "My disreputable ancestor seems to have been a domestic tyrant of the worst kind. I wonder what comes next. I think I must call Alice, for the plot thickens, and she is interested in that 'poor sowle,' as Roger calls her, Roger, by the way, seems to have been an honest fellow, and I hope he stood by his 'dear ladye' to some purpose. I'll go and call Alice to hear the rest of the story."

Mrs. Maynard, however, saved him the trouble, by entering the room at that moment. She had her garden hat on.

"What are you doing, Cecil?" said she, "I want you to come out and see the roses. They are lovely."

"All right," said he, "we'll go by and by. I've something here that will interest you more. You remember that tombstone of Roger Trumball, steward to the noble knight, and so on, that we saw in the churchyard. I've found a sort of diary of his all about that poor second wife of his noble knight, whose fate interests you so much. You had better run your eye over the pages I have read, and then we will go on. There is more to come."

"Why, what a tyrant!" said she, when she had finished reading. "He is every bit as bad as I thought him. You won't defend him now, Cecil?"

"Well, we have not come to a murder yet," said Cecil, "and according to you, he has three standing to his account."

"Three! I should not wonder if there were half a dozen," said she. "I think your Sir Everard was capable of anything. But do let us go on. I am dying to know what happened, and it makes it so real to have it all from the mouth of an actual eyewitness that it is almost as horrible as if it were happening now."

Cecil took up the manuscript again and cast his eye over the next page to that where he left off.

"By heavens!" said he, "we seem coming to a crisis."

85

*March 5, 1662.*—I, Roger Trumball, take up my pen after many months, being in some concern for my safety, but more for that of my dear ladye. For how shall I say it? She is gone, and I know not whither. It is a month now since she disappeared. My master hath made a search for her, but he seemeth not to care to find her. Her own people at Tiptoft Manor are away, and I know not where to seek for them in order to discharge my promise to my dear ladye. The idle jade Madelon flaunteth in ribbons and gay attire and plays the mistress. She says forsooth she is housekeeper. I know not what to think."

*Mar. 10.*—Today happening to be in ye stone gallery, I picked up a glove. "Tis my ladye's' said I.
'What is that?' said my master, who was nearby, 'give it to me'; and he turned it over and threw it on the fire.
'Maybe,' said I, 'she dropped it as she went away.'
My master changed colour and looked hard at me without speaking. 'Went away,' said he. 'perchance you know whither she went and where she is.'
'No, sir,' said I, 'if I knew I would tell you, and if she were in trouble do my best to help her.'
'I doubt you will never find her,' said he looking sourly at me.
'Maybe, sir,' said I, 'you have a better clue than I'
I know not what made me say that; but it had a queer effect. My master turned pale, looked hard at me for the space of a minute, and walked away without a word. I marvelled at his manner."

*Mar. 11.*—I write this from my bed in ye steward's room, being hurt, though not badly. Last night, coming back to the Castle through the woods, I heard a shot, and felt a blow on my leg which brought me to the ground, where I lay till Giles the keeper came in sight, to whom I called for help. 'Why, Master Roger,' quoth he, as he lifted me up, 'what's wrong with you? Why, you bleed like a pig,' and whipping off his handkerchief, he bound up my wound as well as he could, and then leaning on his shoulder, I managed to get home and go to bed, where good Mistress Margery, the still-room maid tended me, and sent for the leech. I saw no man in the wood, and know not of any that beareth me an ill-will. My wound is only slight, but I shall be lame for a while. There is great talk among the servants."

*April 30.*—This day I was summoned to the Hall, where sat my master and with him was Denis Cowley, the farmer of Hay-hill

'Roger,' said my master, speaking quite smooth and gently, 'I have been asking Denis for his quarter's rent, and he says he paid it to you.'

'That is so, ain't it, Master Roger,' said Denis, 'and here is the receipt and your name to it.'

'Quite right,' said I, 'and you will mind, sir, how I handed it on to you the next day.'

'Indeed,' said he, 'I do not mind it; but if so you will have my note of it in your book.'

'I will go this moment and fetch it,' said I, and went to my room. My master was speaking so mildly and gently that I doubted he had some mischief in hand, for he is never so dangerous as when he is in that vein. However, I brought him the book and put it in his hand.

'Well, Roger,' said he, turning over page after page, 'I don't find the note you speak of. You know you always take a note from me to show I have had the money.'

'That is true, sir,' said I. 'Denis's rent is the last entry in the book, and there you will find it. I mind well your writing it in the small parlour, and you putting the money away.'

He looked at me queerly for a minute, and then said, 'take your book then, and find it for yourself.'

But when I looked, the page was gone.

'Have you found it?' he asked.

'Sir, I know not who hath done it, but the page is gone.'

'Indeed,' said he, 'that's odd, but I think it would have been still odder had you found it, for I don't believe it ever was there.'

I was so taken aback that I could find no words for a moment.

'It is not the first time, Roger, I have had my suspicion of you. And now here is honest Master Cowley to prove you had the money, and your book to show you never paid it to me.'

'Sir,' said I, 'you know you had the money. But this seems a plot to ruin me. I'll make the money good if you wish, but I'll never submit to be called a thief.'

'Denis,' said my master, 'you hear him. He admits he took it and will make it good. But,' said he, turning to me, 'that won't clear you. You are a thief, and by god it's a hanging matter if I give you up. If I spare you for a while you will owe it to my mercy. Now go.'

I went slowly to my room, for my lameness still troubled me, and sat down to think it over. I examined the book, and saw how the page had been cut out with a sharp knife. There has been some foul treachery here. *Deliver me. O Lord, from the evil man, and preserve me from the wicked man.* Truly David had his trouble from traitors when he wrote that. As I sat on my bed I thought of all that had befallen me of late: first the wound in my leg, and now this plot for my ruin. My life and my honour were both in danger, but who was my enemy, and who would be the better for my destruction?

I knew my master misliked me for my confidence with his ladye, and then there came into my mind his strange behaviour when I found the glove and spoke with him of my ladye's loss. It was the very night after that that I was shot, and thoughts came into my mind that there might be some link between the two things, but I dare not write no more of this. My master hath me in his power, for who will take my word against his as to the matter of the money.

*June 10.*—Great to do among the servants about Madelon, who is to go to her home. It seems the master has misused her, and she would have none of it, and so she is to leave. I fear I have misjudged the girl, and that she is better than I thought of her. This day I happened on her coming out of my room. I was surprised, for she had no call to be there. She had been crying, and I spoke to her kindly.

'Why, mistress Madelon,' said I, 'I hear you are going, but that should not grieve you; you will be well out of this house.'

'Indeed I shall, master Roger. I would I had never entered it. I have been made to do things I am ashamed of, and am sorry for now. And for some of them I cannot now make amends; it is too late.'

'Why so, Madelon?'

'Nay, you know very well,' said she, 'I mean my mistress.'

'I know,' said I, 'you were set to spy on her by my master.'

'I was,' she said; 'he made me, and I'm sorry I did it.'

'And do you know where she is,' said I, 'and what has happened to her?'

Madelon looked round and waited to know if anyone were within hearing before she answered in a whisper.

'Nay, I know not, though I can make guess, and I think he suspects me. I hate him, Roger, and will do him a mischief if I can, for he has treated me vilely.' Here we heard footsteps approaching, and the girl said in haste:

'I know you love me not, Master Roger, but I have been a better friend to you than you know of,' and with that she ran away.

My master has said nothing more to me about the money, but I can see he views me with an evil eye. My leg troubles me sorely, and I doubt I am lamed for life, though I can ride, and get about with a stick well enough. I have no news yet of Sir Charles or his sons, and it vexes me that I cannot perform what I promised my dear ladye, but I have sworn on the Holy Bible that I will perform it, and that, alive or dead, I will make known unto them what she suffered before we lost her, and what has since befallen her should I find out.

"I wonder," said Alice, as Cecil laid down the manuscript for a minute, "whether poor Roger ever did find the Tiptofts and redeem his promise."

"We shall have Henry Tiptoft here in a day or two," said Cecil, "and he may be able to tell us something about it. But I fancy they know as little over there of the story of poor Hilda as I did till I happened on this account in the *County History* which set us all on this quest."

"Well, go on," said she. "I hope poor Roger came to no harm from that murderous master of his."

Cecil resumed the reading:

*June 15.*—A strange thing happened today. I was receiving rents from two or three tenants for their farms, and giving them receipts. It was the first time this had happened since the affair of Master Denis Cowley, and this time I resolved there should be no handle for my master's malice, and that in future the book in which he noted that I paid him the money should be kept in a more secure place under lock and key. So I put the money in a bag, and took down my notebook, and opened it, and a piece of paper flew out upon the floor.

When I picked it up I saw it was the missing leaf, with my master's receipt on it. I was so taken aback that I sat down again to think it over, for I was fairly overcome. Then I bethought me of Madelon, and how surprised her coming out of my room, and of her words at parting, and it was borne in upon me that she had cut the page out at her master's bidding, and had kept it for future service if needs should be, and had put it back when her master had offended her. I blessed the girl in my heart and forgave her for what she first did, and I rejoiced to feel that my master had no longer that hold over me. I saw plainly it had been a plot to get me into his power, so that I should not be able to stir hand or foot against him for fear of the gallows.

But what had I against him? I bethought me of that I said to him about my ladye's loss when I found the glove, which might have made him think I suspected him of something wrong. But he had no reason, for I knew nothing then, and I know nothing now about my poor ladye's fate. And then it was borne in upon me that perhaps he knew more about it than he would have me suspect. I begin to fear that there has been some foul play, and I then remembered Madelon's last words. I must see her again.

However, after a while I recovered myself and taking my notebook and the money, I sought my master in the great library, where it was his pleasure to sit. I told him I had brought the rents and I laid them on the table that he might count them, and I spread the notebook open before him that he might enter his receipt. When he had signed his name, he said:

'This time you are right, Roger. Last time you made a little mistake, if I remember.'

'Sir Everard,' said I, 'I know not what you mean. If there were a mistake 'twas not I that made it.'

'A little mistake,' said he, smiling, 'that brought you within danger of the gallows, eh, Master Roger.'.

'Nay, sir,' I replied, quite coolly, ''twas not I that was in danger of the gallows. I mind me there is a law to punish those that plot to ruin their fellows by false charges.'

He turned furiously on me. I wonder I had the courage to threaten him as I did. But I was mad with anger.

'Plot and punishment,' cried he. 'You dare to accuse and threaten me, gallows-bird; to jail you shall go this day and stay there till the hangman is ready for you.'

'You charge me with stealing the money, though you had it fairly from me, and gave me your receipt,' said I.

'Show me the receipt then,' cried he savagely. 'You know you have not got one.'

I took from my pocket the loose leaf I found in my book and held it before him.

'Give it me,' he cried.

'Nay,' said I, 'it shall not leave me again.'

He sank back in his seat. The blood rushed to his face, and he sat staring at me with his mouth open for the space of a minute. At last he began to stammer out a word or two of excuse, but he could hardly speak for shame and mortification. I gathered up my books and papers, but as I turned to go I heard him mutter to himself, 'the jade—played me false.'

I fear I have angered my master beyond sufferance, and that he may take some vengeance upon me, for he is one that never forgives, though he smoothes his anger over with fair pretence. I bethink me of that shot in the wood, and doubt I am in some danger of my life. I pray God I may live to find my ladye, and to fulfil the promise to which I have sworn. *Deliver me from mine enemies, O God, defend me from them that rise up against me.*

*June 23.*—This morning I found on my writing desk a note written in a hand that I knew not, and none of the servants could say how it came there. It was written in a crabbed style by one who was no scribe.

'To Master Roger Trumball,

'these

'Look to yourself, there is mischief determined against you. Where you found the glove you may find more. Sir Charles is home.—M.'

I take it this comes from Madelon. It is a kind lass and I thank her. I must be careful.

Today I had occasion to speak with my master on business. Since the matter of the receipt note he hath avoided me, though when we meet he treateth me civilly. I found him today in the stone gallery. There were two masons there, and work going on. Some furniture had been moved, and I saw a hole in the wall, which was being built up. I had never noticed it before, and indeed a cabinet had stood in front, and I was curious to see what it was. My master seemed anxious to prevent me, and stood in my way. It was dark within, and I thought I saw a door some way back, but my master called me away with him to the other part of the room, and, as the cabinet that had been moved out stood across, I could see no more what was behind it. My master said he had long been troubled with a draught from that empty cupboard, and was having it walled up. When I had discharged my business I said to him:

'sir, they say Sir Charles Tiptoft hath made terms with the government, and is now at home. Would you that I ride and tell him of my ladye? I doubt he knows not of her loss, for he has been in jail till now.'

'No!' said he, 'let him find it out for himself. I will have no dealings with malcontents and roundheads.'

This put me out, for I had hoped to have seen my ladye's family and to have discharged my trust. So I went about my business as usual till after noon. In the evening my master sent for me. I found him walking up and down the library, and he seemed in a good humour.'

'Roger,' he said, 'I think you were right this morning and I was wrong about Sir Charles. It is true we were on different sides in politics, and during the war enemies, but that is all happily over, and we must now live in good fellowship as neighbours. He ought to know about my poor wife, which will grieve him as it grieves me, and you will ride over tomorrow and tell him of her sad and strange departure, and of our failure to find out whither she has gone.'

I was much surprised to hear him talk in this way, for he had never shown much love for my dear ladye while she was with him.

'What time will you start?' asked he.

I said I would start about ten o'clock next morning.

'And which way will you go?'

I said the nighest way would be by Langford and Chaldicote.

'Aye, aye,' said he, 'that will take you through the woods, and be pleasant riding this summer weather, it is hot, and tomorrow you know is Midsummer Day. I would not ride fast if I were you, but take it slowly.'

I said I took it kindly of him to think of me so, and that I was sure sir Charles would be much grieved by my news. 'Truly, I think so,' said he. 'You start then, at ten o'clock tomorrow morning. Do not be later. And you go through Langford and Chaldicote, by way of the forest. I wish you a pleasant ride. Be sure and see me when you come back.'

So I took my leave, marvelling much at his pleasant humour, and yet somehow mistrusting him, for I knew him to be treacherous. As I reached the door, I turned and saw him looking at me with a strange smile on his face that I did not like.

So tomorrow I shall tell all I know to my ladye's kin, as I have sworne, and yet it cometh not to much, though I suspect a good deal. Alive or dead, I have sworne, and I know I shall keep my oath. Yet I like not my master's manner. Why so nice about my road and about the hour? The wood was where I was shot. I will be wary, and go armed. And as I shall be away it will be safer if I hide these records of my dealings with my master and my ladye in some place where they may not be found, should ought befall me, till this tyranny be overpast.

Tomorrow is Midsummer Day. Today is what the Papists called St. John's Eve, when all enchantments come undone, and the truth appears. Would that it might reveal the truth of what befell my dear Ladye.

Here Cecil stopped.

"Well, go on," said his wife. "We can't stop here. I wonder

how he fared on his ride."

"That's all," said Cecil. "There is no more."

They looked at one another.

"Do you remember," said Cecil, "the date on poor Roger's tombstone?"

"Yes," said she. "I do. I remember it was June 24, 1662. I particularly remember noticing that it was Midsummer Day."

"And this was written on Midsummer Eve," said Cecil, "so poor Roger never got to Tiptoft Manor, and has never yet been able to keep his promise."

Flaming June was more than half spent when Sir Henry Tiptoft drove up to Castle Maynard, and was welcomed in the hall by his host and hostess. The luncheon bell was ringing, and as soon as the visitor had been shown his room, and washed off the dust of travel, they sat down in the cool oak-panelled dining-room, overlooking the old-fashioned garden. It was the last addition to the house, built in the time of George II., with tall panels reaching up to the ceiling, and a wide marble chimneypiece placed cornerwise across one angle. A room stately and yet homely, not unlike a Common-room at Oxford.

The talk was such as was natural between old friends—Oxford memories, local gossip, speculations concerning the harvest and hay-crop—and after luncheon they adjourned to the garden, and had coffee on the terrace, with a lovely view of park and river, a real English landscape, green and lush. The old house, too, was typically English, and could have been in no other land, a mixture of splendour and homeliness, state and comfort. The main part was Jacobean, of red brick, mellowed by time, with many gables, mullioned windows and projecting bays.

But at the end was a considerable part of the old castle of Plantagenet times, finished at the river brink with a huge round tower that rose above the highest roof, and was the most conspicuous feature in the structure. As the ground fell steeply towards the river, the tower descended some twenty feet below the ground level and the terrace in front of the rest of the house. The old part was built of flint and wrought stone, with windows enlarged to comfortable dimensions from the original arrow-slits.

Henry Tiptoft was as yet a bachelor, but was to be married shortly. He had passed through Oxford with distinction, and was already making his mark in the county as an able magistrate, and it was thought he meant to contest the seat in Parliament. His tastes, however, were rather literary and scientific than such as make the ardent politician. While an undergraduate at Merton, he had published at his own expense a small volume of poems, of which he was now heartily ashamed, and since then had made some more successful efforts in prose.

He was a bit of an antiquary and a student of history. His poetical vein had not been dried up by his early failure; his imagination was strong and active, and not a little touched with sentiment. Castle Maynard appealed to him strongly and roused him to enthusiasm.

"I had not realised," said he, "what a wonderful old home you have. My old house is not bad, about the date of your Jacobean part, but your remains of the old *château fort* is beyond anything at Tiptoft."

"Yes; it's not a bad old place, is it," said Cecil. "I'm very fond of it, and have been amusing myself since I came here with trying to learn all about its history."

"That's well," said his friend; "it shows you deserve to own it. I can't understand how any man of intelligence can live in an old historical place without hunting up all that can be known about it. I've been doing a bit in that way at Tiptoft, but you have more ample material here and a longer history."

"We have only just discovered that we have a ghost," said Mrs. Maynard. "For a long time I thought there wasn't one, and I was quite disappointed."

"Really! And have you seen it? And pray, whose ghost is it?"

"Why, it's rather funny, Sir Henry, that you should ask me that question, for the ghost is one of your own family."

"Indeed! You interest me greatly. I am a profound believer in ghosts, and never miss a meeting of the Psychical Society," said he, laughing. "But tell me, who of my family is it that favours you with a visit, Mrs. Maynard?"

"Did you ever hear of a Hilda Tiptoft in the time of Charles II., who was married to Sir Everard Maynard?"

"Why, I think I have now you mention it. Was there not some tragedy about it?"

"Quite right," said Cecil. "She was lost, or ran away, or at all events she disappeared, and my wife will have it her husband murdered her."

"Why, Cecil, you know he did," said she.

"I confess things look rather black against him," said Cecil. "But we haven't quite got to the bottom of that story. However, at all events, we have convicted him of murdering another person. I have evidence enough to hang my respectable ancestor if I had him here."

"Well, every family has its black sheep," said Sir Henry. "I dare say we Tiptofts have not always been angels. But where did you get all this story from? You speak as if you had made a discovery."

"So we have, Sir Henry," said Mrs. Maynard. "You must get Cecil to show you the papers we have found, written by an eye witness of Sir Everard's atrocities."

"Not quite that," said Cecil, laughing. "A man can hardly be summoned as an eyewitness of his own murder. And we are not quite sure yet that Sir Everard really murdered anyone else."

"I was in hope," said Mrs. Maynard, "that sir Henry would have been able to help us to clear the matter up. But I fear he knows nothing about it."

"No! I am sorry to say that, beyond a vague idea that there was a mystery about poor Hilda Tiptoft, I know nothing more. But I should like, of all things, to see the papers you have found if I may be allowed to do so."

"By all means, my dear Henry," said Cecil. "In fact we have been looking forward to your doing so, in hope you may throw some light on the mystery. To speak seriously, it is really a gruesome story, and told as it is first hand, I shall confess it made an unpleasant impression on me, although it all happened so long ago. But you shall see the papers and judge for yourself."

They had tea under the trees by the river at the foot of the great tower, at which Tiptoft looked with interest.

"What is there in the lower part of this great tower?" said he. "It is a whole storey below the rest of the house."

"Nothing at all, so far as I know," said Cecil.

"That's disappointing," said Sir Henry. "I thought at least some crusading Maynard had a dungeon there where he kept captive Jews like Front-de-Bœuf, and drew their teeth in order to extract their gold."

"No. I fancy it is solid," said Cecil. "At all events, if there is anything inside there's no way of getting into it."

After tea some neighbours dropped in, and there was tennis, and then they dined, and after dinner they sat on the terrace, and the men smoked and talked till far into the pleasant night before they went to bed.

The next few days were spent in the way usual at a country house. There was fishing and a little rabbit shooting, and a villagers' cricket match, where the captaincy of the blacksmith, Maynard and Tiptoft helped Castle Maynard to beat a rival eleven from Chaldicote. And it was not till the day before Midsummer that Henry Tiptoft recollected the papers, of which he had been promised a view. It was a rainy morning, and he thought he could not spend the time more agreeably than in reading them.

They were produced from the muniment-room and spread out in order on the table in the library, and Cecil, who had business to attend to, left his friend to amuse himself till the evening. Scarcely, however, had he settled himself comfortably at the table with the prospect of an interesting historical research, exactly to his taste, before Mrs. Maynard made demands on his company, and then after luncheon they went for a ride, and it was not till after tea that he at last sat down quietly to enjoy Roger Trumball's diary.

Cecil Maynard did not get back till just before dinner, and had only time to dress and join his wife and his friend in the great hall before they were marshalled by the butler into the dining-room. During dinner Henry was rather silent and abstracted, and left his host and hostess to carry on most of the conversation. Cecil had been at the quarter sessions, and was full of stories and episodes of the proceedings, and Mrs. Maynard had much to say of village matters and local politics, and so they hardly noticed the change in their guest's manner.

It was not till Mrs. Maynard had retired leaving them on the terrace smoking, that Cecil was struck by Sir Henry's silence, and could not help asking him whether anything was amiss.

"I'm glad you asked me," said Tiptoft, "I've been longing to tell you, but I could not speak of it while Mrs. Maynard was here for fear of frightening her."

"Why, what has happened?" said Cecil in some alarm.

"I've been reading those papers you showed me," said he. "They leave off abruptly, and there cannot be much doubt that he was in danger on that ride of his. Do you know anything further about it?"

"I do, indeed. You may have noticed that the last page was dated June 23, 1662, the date of his ride to his death, June 24, 1662, the day following."

"I see. You mean that he was murdered on his way. The ride was a plot of his master to get rid of him?"

"Just so. And the tombstone must have been put up by his murderer. He suspected Roger of scheming to expose him, and so sent him to his death and wrote on his tombstone *There is no device in the grave whither thou goest.* Can you conceive a more ghastly piece of Satanic humour?"

"Devilish, indeed. But do you remember why Roger wanted to go to Tiptoft?"

"I remember," said Cecil. "it was to tell your people how his poor mistress had been treated, and had disappeared, and no doubt to hint at some foul play so as to put an inquiry on foot."

"He says he had promised his dear lady he would do this, living or dead, and that he had sworn it on the Holy Bible, if you remember."

"I remember," said Cecil. "But, poor fellow, he did not live to fulfil his promise."

"He says living or dead," replied Tiptoft.

"What do you mean?" said Cecil, looking at him after a pause.

"He has fulfilled it," said Henry.

There was silence for a few minutes. At last recovering his composure which had been much disturbed, Henry continued:

"I'll tell you exactly what happened. You know I was in the library? Well, as I read poor Roger Trumball's story I became more and more absorbed. It seemed to fascinate me in a way I had never experienced before. It was as if the scene were before me; as if it was being enacted now, and by living men and women, instead of having happened nearly three hundred years ago by those who are now dust and ashes. It laid hold of me in such a way that I seemed to lose my own identity, and be a mere visionary spectator of a horrible drama; of scenes in which, though I was present, I was powerless to act.

"A sense of something supernatural came over me, unseen influences seemed around me, and as I finished the last page I sat a few minutes trying in vain to collect my faculties. At last I rose from my chair, and leaving the manuscript open upon the table, I walked to the fireplace. I looked round the room. This was the place, I said to myself, where the scene took place between Roger and his master, when he confounded him by producing the missing receipt.

"This was the room, too, where the last scene in the story was enacted, and I seemed to see Sir Everard with his devilish hypocritical *bonhomie* laying the trap for his victim's death, and poor Roger, loyal to his mistress, falling into the trap, not without some misgivings, but resolved at all hazards to fulfil his promise to tell all he knew to the Tiptofts. He had sworn he would do it, living or dead. I found myself saying aloud almost unconsciously, 'living or dead; living or dead.'

"At that moment I happened to turn my eye towards the

place where I had been sitting. That part of the room was in shadow, and the evening was beginning to set in, but I saw at the table a figure standing and seeming to look at the papers that lay there, Thinking it was a servant come to arrange the room, for I did not see him vey distinctly, I said, 'Please do not disturb those papers; I will attend to them.'

"As he took no notice, I repeated what I said. The figure slowly turned and looked at me. Something seemed to seize me by the throat and stop my speech, and I could only look at him in silence. The face was grave, and the expression god and kindly. He seemed a man of middle age, strongly built, dressed in sober brown or grey, but I did not much notice his dress, for his face fascinated me. He took up the last page of the diary and put his finger on the bottom line, and then laid it down. A noise at the other end of the room startled me, and I looked round. When I turned my head again he was gone. I looked at the line to which he pointed. These were the words: *Alive or dead, I have sworne, and I know I shall keep my oath.*"

The two men sat silent for a while, and then Cecil said:

"A strange story. You, I know, are a believer in psychical phenomena. I am not. Forgive my asking, but are you quite sure it was not a dream? It is exactly what one might dream after having been excited as you were by this gruesome story. I felt something like you myself as I read it, and had to keep thinking to myself this is all ancient history, the actors are gone and turned to dust, and the sinners have paid the penalty of their misdeeds, long long ago."

"I don't wonder at your doubt, my dear Cecil. In your place I might doubt too. But believe me, it was no dream, for there was no awaking. I remember walking out of the library to my bedroom quite distinctly, and I can recall all that passed till we met at dinner. No. Roger swore to take his message to a Tiptoft, and he has, I firmly believe, fulfilled his promise."

"Well, *there are more things in heaven and earth*—you know the rest," said Cecil. "And now, I see, you are shaken and want a good night's rest, so let us go."

But Tiptoft could not rest when he got to his bedroom. His nerves were shaken and still in a flutter. If it had really been a vision, and not, as Maynard supposed a dream, what did it mean? What was to follow? It could hardly have been allowed without a purpose, and the matter could not end here. He walked to the window and leaned out. The moon was high in the clear summer sky, and touched the landscape with magic light. The old crusading tower shone out white and brilliantly against the dark trees beyond the river, of which the gentle murmur as it broke over its rock bed, was the only sound audible.

Henry thought of all those ancient walls had witnessed, of good and evil, joy and sorrow, of crime and mystery, of Sir Everard and poor Roger Trumball, and of the pitiful lady whose fate was unknown, and whose blood ran in his veins. A strange fancy possessed him that Roger had bequeathed the quest to him, and that it was his part to solve the mystery of Hilda Tiptoft. In vain did he pooh! Pooh! The idea, and say with Cecil, that it was all ancients history, that the actors, both sinners and victims had long been dissolved into their native earth.

The narrative he had read made it all alive again. How was the matter to be brought to light? And then there came into his mind Roger's words about Midsummer Eve, and the Popish superstition that all enchantments were dissolved and truth revealed on St. John's Eve. And, by heavens, it was Midsummer Day tomorrow, and this was St. John's Eve, the anniversary of poor Roger's last entry in his diary before he went to his death. How strange the coincidence. Could it be that tonight was to solve the mystery of the past three hundred years? A desire seized him to read the words again. The manuscript, he knew, was still lying on the library table; it was near midnight and everybody would be asleep, and he could get what he wanted without disturbing the house.

As he turned to leave the window his eyes fell on the old Crusader's tower, and in the lower part he saw a light glimmering from a narrow slit where Cecil had said there was no room, but only solid masonry. This surprised him, as he remembered afterwards, but at the time his thoughts were elsewhere. The queer sense of a supernatural presence that had weighed upon him in the afternoon was upon him again. Unseen influences seemed again to surround him and he was almost in a trance when he reached the library door and laid his hand on the latch. He did not enter, for something moving a little way down the corridor caught his eye.

It was in the shadow now, but beyond was a patch of moonlight from a window, and whatever it was, it was bound to cross it. Surprise and alarm recalled some of his scattered wits, when he saw distinctly the figure of a man creeping stealthily with silent footfall along the wall. He seemed dressed in black and had something in his hand that for a moment caught the moonlight and glittered. There was some ancient weapons hanging on the walls, and Henry instinctively grasped an old pistol from among them, the first thing his hand fell upon, and then followed as quietly as he could. The man led him through several passages to an old part of the castle, where he had never been before.

The moonlight that entered here and there only made the rest of the way darker by contrast, but Henry was able to keep the man in view. They were now in a long gallery, imperfectly lit, for it did not face the moon, and the man suddenly disappeared. Putting out his hand and feeling along the wall he found an opening, a doorway it seemed, low and narrow, and looking down he saw a faint light below and a narrow stairway descending. The man was before him, moving strangely quietly, for his footsteps were inaudible. Henry was drawn in by an irresistible impulse to follow. The man never looked round and was apparently quite unaware he was being followed. The stair ended in a room, round, low and vaulted.

There was a table and a lamp on it, shedding a feeble light, and at the table, with her head on her hand and her face towards him, sat a beautiful woman. The man was hidden in the passage and she did not see him, but Henry could look clearly over his shoulder. They remained thus some minutes, and then the woman rose, fell on her knees at the table, her head sank on her clasped hands and she seemed in prayer. Her back was towards them. And now the man stole softly forward towards her and in his hand was the long dagger that had glittered in the moonlight. In another moment he would be upon her, his hand was raised, when some spell seemed to break. Henry found his tongue and cried aloud. The man turned and looked at him for a moment and Henry saw his face distinctly. It was not the face of a living man, but of a benevolent demon.

The man said nothing, but advanced upon him with the dagger raised. Henry snapped the pistol at him, but of course in vain, for it was unloaded, a fact that in his dreamy state had not occurred to him. He flung the empty pistol at his assailant without effect, for he still came on; there was a chair close by, and hurling that in his enemy's path, Henry fled up the stair. He was pursued, but reaching the top found a door, which he slammed to behind him, and ran breathless till he reached the main staircase, on which he fell with a cry and remembered no more.

The cry brought out Cecil, who found his friend in a faint. Assistance was called, and Henry was put to bed. He was not in a condition to answer any questions, and indeed, seemed in such a state of terror that he could not be left alone. The diabolical face haunted him; he could not get it out of his mind; he raved in a semi-delirious state for some hours, while Cecil stood by him, wondering much what disaster had overtaken him, and when at last sleep came to him, he still seemed to find terror in his dreams.

It was a week after this that the two friends were sitting in the garden, Henry Tiptoft, still somewhat pale and out of sorts, for he had suffered a severe shock. Mrs. Maynard was sitting with them, and Henry Tiptoft had for the first time found courage to tell his experience of that fateful night. They had listened with amazement and some incredulity.

"But, my dear Henry," said Cecil, "you must have dreamt it, for there is no place in the castle in the least like what you describe."

"Perhaps not now," said Tiptoft, "but there may have been.

What I saw, remember, was in image of what took place nearly three hundred years ago. That at least, is how I understand it. It was borne in upon me, to use the expression poor Roger Trumball was so fond of, that I was destined to discover the fate of his poor lady, and that he came for that purpose to pass the quest on to my shoulders. I believe what I saw was what really happened: that the lady was imprisoned in some vault in the castle, and murdered there by her husband, in order to get possession of the whole of her estate it would seem."

"You saw the man's face, you say. Should you know it again?"

"Know it! I shall never forget it."

"Well then, you shall come to the picture gallery and see whether you can pick out Sir Everard from the rest, and identify him with your vision. That would be very interesting."

"Yes, but I see you are still incredulous and think I dreamed it all. The only thing to convince you will be to find the stair and the vault."

"Do you remember," said Mrs. Maynard, "Roger says he found Sir Everard with workmen engaged in walling up a doorway?"

"By Jove, Alice," said Cecil, "so he did. That seems to afford a clue. But he said it was in the stone gallery, and there is no place in the house known by that name, or answering to it."

"It comes back to me," said Henry, "that I saw a light glimmering from a slit in the lower part of the old tower which you said was solid with nothing inside. Now I think I can see something like an arrow slit behind the ivy."

Some ivy was pulled down, and a narrow window was exposed and Cecil was obliged to confess that so far, at all events, he was wrong. There might be a vault then, if sir Henry's vision was to be depended upon, in the old tower, of which the existence had been forgotten.

"The stone gallery must be that passage which leads to my *boudoir* on the ground floor of the old tower, and if there is a vault, my *boudoir* must be over it," said Mrs. Maynard, and she guided them to it. The *boudoir* was a round room with a lovely view, but Mrs. Maynard said if it was over any horror she should never like it again. The problem now, was to find the doorway which Roger saw being blocked. Workmen were sent for, and after a careful examination a piece of walling was detected as an insertion, by the experienced eye of the clerk of works. Behind was found a doorway and a stair. Lights were brought and the two men descended. Henry went first. At the foot of the stair he uttered an exclamation.

"Don't let Mrs. Maynard come down Cecil," said he, "I don't want her to see it."

In the vault, among cobwebs and dust beside an old table, lay a heap of something indefinite, some remains of drapery and linen, yellow with age; and among them, all that was left of poor Hilda Tiptoft.

She was found at last.

It may be added in conclusion, that Sir Henry Tiptoft was taken to the gallery and unhesitantly picked out the portrait of Sir Everard, though some might say he had the costume of the seventeenth century to help him.

"But the curious thing about it," said Maynard, "is that I picked up an old pistol in the vault just like the one that hangs in the hall."

"Then," said Sir Henry, "perhaps now you will believe that my vision was not a dream."

But Cecil said, "I must first go and see if there is one missing from the hall."

# Pepina

The assizes were being held in the county town, and between the rising of the Court and the time for the Bar mess at the "Bull's Head" a few hours were available for a little pleasant exercise. The surrounding country was pretty and inviting, and offered many field-walks, and two members of the Bar, taking advantage of the summer evening, might have been seen strolling along a woodland path a mile or two from the town. Their demeanour, however, was not in keeping with the peaceful scenery, for there were angry words between them.

The elder of the two was a man of fine presence, and a distinguished air. His countenance was expressive of power and determination. He seemed a man who would have his own way whatever it might cost others, but with due allowance for its selfishness, it was not altogether a bad face. He looked like a man easy to get on with if you did not cross him. His companion was a good deal younger, his countenance was frank and open, intelligent and kindly, though at this moment it was clouded with displeasure.

"But I don't understand you," said the elder. "What do you object to?"

"I've told you, Sir Edward," said the younger man, "that your addresses to my sister must be discontinued. I cannot consent to their going on."

"But, my dear Cranston, you are not your sister's keeper. I am, of course, very sorry you disapprove, but your sister, I am sanguine enough to think, does not agree with you. At all events, she has not discouraged me."

"She does not know all I do about you, or she would think as I do. I do not think you are fit for her, and as her brother, I object to the alliance."

"Indeed," said the other with some hauteur, "I should have thought an Attorney-General good enough for the sister of a junior barrister."

"You know very well that is not what I mean. Think of your past. Have you forgotten Naples and Pepina?"

"Oh!" said Sir Edward Wilson in some confusion, "you are going to rake up that story. Of course, I remember Pepina, though I dare say she has forgotten me. It must be three years ago—"

"Then you do not know what became of her? It was like you never to inquire."

"Well, no; we parted in a hurry, and—"

"And what? You meanly through her off after ruining her, and broke her heart," said Cranston. "Shall I tell you the rest?"

"Well!" said Sir Edward. "What is it?"

"The morning after you brutally turned her adrift and left Naples, her body was found in the canal."

Sir Edward, much shocked, said nothing for a minute. Then recollecting himself, he stammered out:

"I am very sorry. I had no idea she—well—yes, I am really distressed, but—"

"But, you are going to say, it was not your fault. I tell you her blood lies at your door. I wonder her spirit does not haunt you. Let me tell you one thing more. The last thing she did before she threw herself into the water was to send me a note. I have it still. It only contained these words:

"'*Dica al traditore, ti rivedro all' ora giusta.—*Pepina'"

"Cranston," said Sir Edward, recovering himself, "this is a sad story, but it is past and gone and cannot be helped. It is unkind of you to revive it."

"And do you think my sister would marry you if she knew

it?"

"But she need never know it."

"That depends on you," said Cranston.

"What do you mean?"

"She shall know it if you continue your addresses."

"Do you mean you will tell her?" said he in rising passion.

"I do."

"By Heaven," said he, standing in front of him, "you shall not!"

"Then I understand you mean to persevere," said Cranston. "She shall know it this very night," and he turned on his heel to go homewards.

The other held him, and Cranston, unable to release himself, struck him; the blow was returned, and in a moment they were locked in a deadly struggle. They were not unequally matched, for if one were the stronger the other was younger and more active, but at last Cranston stumbled and fell, and the other, seizing a stick that lay handy, struck him on the head once and again, and then stood panting and looking at his fallen foe.

Cranston did not move. The victor grew anxious and bent over him. "Cranston, for God's sake, my dear fellow, speak to me. I did not mean it, speak to me," cried he in agony.

The dying man opened his eyes and looked at him; in a whisper came the words, "I leave you to Pepina."

Sir Edward Wilson felt all the horror of his position. It had not been a fair fight; that last blow made it a murder. What was to be done? The wood was thick, and the body might be hidden for a time at all events. He dragged it into a thicket and hid it as well as he could, and then rearranging his disordered dress, returned to the town

There was nothing noticeable in his manner as he sat at the bar dinner except that he was more silent than usual, for generally his brilliant talk and caustic wit made him the arbiter of the conversation. It was thought he was fatigued, for he had conducted a very important case that day in court.

"What has become of Cranston?" said someone. "He'll get

no dinner unless he looks sharp. Did he not go out with you, Sir Edward?"

"Yes," said he. "We started together, but he went beyond me and I came back alone."

"I'm told," said another, "it's not very safe just now to wander about in these woods. The miners are out on strike, and they say several people have been stopped and robbed—"

"Oh! Cranston's able to take care of himself," said a third. "I don't think he will come to any harm."

And then the matter was forgotten, and other topics came up.

But next morning, when a cause came on in which Cranston was engaged, he was missing, and it was found on inquiry that he had not been at his lodgings. Telegrams were sent to his friends, who replied they knew nothing of his movements. People began to be alarmed, and search was made in the neighbourhood. It was not, however, till the third day that the Press was able to make the following announcement:—

We regret to have to report that the mystery attaching the disappearance of Mr. Philip Cranston, a barrister attending circuit in this town, has been solved in the most tragic manner. The body of the unfortunate gentleman was found yesterday in the neighbouring woods under circumstances indicating that a foul murder has been committed. Evidences were apparent of a struggle, and a bludgeon was discovered with blood and hair on it, evidently the instrument of this atrocious deed. The body had been rifled of all valuables, watch and chain were gone, and the pockets were turned out, showing that robbery was the motive for this dastardly crime. We take this opportunity of reminding our readers that several cases of robbery in the neighbourhood have occurred recently, and it would seem that the police have been singularly lax in their surveillance. We understand the inquest will be held on Tuesday.

The inquest was held, but there was little evidence to put

before the jury. The policeman who found the body told his story, and sir Edward was called as having been the last person in his company, but he only repeated what he had said before at dinner, and the jury returned a verdict of "Wilful murder against some person or persons unknown," accompanied with a recommendation to the police to be more careful. Many of Cranston's friends attended the inquest, including the judge himself, and there was much discussion about the matter afterwards, as they walked away.

"What puzzles me," said one, "is why Mr. Attorney and Cranston went out for a walk together. I know Cranston did not like him."

"Nonsense," said the other, "Everyone knows Wilson wants to marry Cranston's sister."

"I fancy that is not settled," replied his friend; "I know Cranston objected. He has never been friendly with Wilson since that time they went to Italy together three years ago. Something or other happened to make a breach between them, but I believe it was Cranston who took offence and not Wilson."

"However, they went out for a walk together that day anyhow, which looks friendly."

"Yes," said the other. "Wilson was the last man seen in his company."

"Why, you don't mean—" said the other laughing.

"No, no, I mean nothing, but it's rather funny, isn't it?"

The assizes were over. The judge was gone to the next county town, and the Bar was following. The Attorney-General returned to town to attend to his Parliamentary duties. As he sat alone in the railway carriage with nothing to occupy him, the full horror of what had happened rushed in upon him. The scene in the wood; the struggle; the fatal last blow. Would to god he had not yielded to that mad homicidal impulse. And Cranston had been his chosen friend and companion; he had in his selfish way loved him. To think he should have slain him!

And Lucy Cranston. How could he face her with her brother's blood on his hands? That at all events was all over now. As to discovery, he felt safe. The robbery of the body diverted suspicion in a wrong direction, and the thief would be silent for his own sake. He had at first thought of telling the truth, and taking his chance; but then there was his position at the head of his profession, with the highest prize almost in his grasp, and to confess to a murderous brawl, and stand his trial for manslaughter meant ruin in any case, and was not to be thought of. At all events, it was too late now; things had gone too far. And then he thought of Pepina.

Her blood too, as Cranston said, lay at his door. Two deaths stood against him in the great account. He was a selfish, but not naturally cruel man, and the horror of it almost stunned him. "Good God!" he cried, "What have I done to bring all this upon me?" He thought of pretty Pepina, as he first saw her, an innocent and happy rustic beauty in the vineyard near Naples. Of her love and trust in him, and of his desertion of her. He hated himself as he thought of it, and would have made any conceivable atonement; but the time for that was past; she was dead, and he had to bear the guilt of her death. What did her last message mean? He was to see her again at the right time. When would that be? Though a sceptic as to things supernatural, he felt afraid.

And then Cranston's dying words recurred to him, "I leave you to Pepina." They fastened a creeping terror upon him, and seemed burned into his brain. He felt they would never leave him. That day and night the thought of Pepina would recur to him, and perhaps drive him mad.

But Sir Edward Wilson was a man of strong self-command; when the train drew into the terminus he was able to recover himself, and when he met his household he showed no traces of the ordeal he had gone through.

Six months had slipped away, and few but those who loved him ever thought of the murder of Philip Cranston, though it made a stir at the time. Two ladies in deep mourning were sitting in a pleasant drawing-room in the West end of London, looking out on the Square garden, where the trees were just burgeoning into fresh life after their winter' sleep.

"Lucy," said the elder lady, "did I tell you Sir Edward Wilson called about a fortnight ago for the first time after poor Philip's death. You will remember how kindly he wrote about it at the time. He asked about you, but I think you were out."

"No, I was not out. But I did not wish to see him."

Mrs. Cranston laid down her work and looked at her daughter in some surprise. After a pause she continued:

"I may be wrong, Lucy, but I fancied you did not discourage his addresses. All our friends seemed to think it would be a match."

"Oh, no, indeed, mother," said Lucy. "There is nothing between us. He has said nothing to me, and I hope he never will, for I could not listen to his proposals, and should be sorry to have to refuse him."

"And yet he has much to offer. He is at the head of his profession, with a brilliant career before him. But, of course, if you don't like him well enough to marry him, you are right to avoid him."

"No, mother, with all his brilliant career, and all that, I could never marry him. To tell you the truth, I am afraid of him. I think he is an idolater, and the idol he worships is himself, and he is prepared to sacrifice to his idol everything that stands in his way."

"You think him selfish and unscrupulous?"

"Yes. I think any woman who married him would have to be either his slave or his victim, and I have no wish to be either."

"And yet you remember he was dear Philip's most intimate friend at one time. They travelled together in Italy only three years ago."

"That is true, but I know Philip did not like him so well lately. Something or other happened on that tour that made Philip distrust him. He never said anything to me about it, but I could see that he did not like Sir Edward's coming here so often."

There was silence for a little while, and then Lucy said:

"I have often wondered what it was that offended Philip,

for I know he was attached to Sir Edward formerly, and had an unbounded admiration for his talents. You know I have been looking over his old letter and papers, and I thought I might find something there to throw light upon it, but I found nothing, unless one curious scrap, written in Italian, has anything to do with it. I did not destroy it with other papers that seemed not worth keeping and which I tore up, for it seemed rather curious. I will go and fetch it, for I should like you to see it."

She went to her room and came back with a piece of paper in her hand, and gave it to her mother. It had been folded as a note and sealed, and was addressed on the outside in an illiterate hand to *Signor Filippo, Inglese*. Mrs. Cranston read it thoughtfully, and laid it on her lap. After a while she said to her daughter:

"It is very curious, Lucy. '*Dica al traditore ti rivedro all' ora giusta.*' 'Tell the traitor I shall see him again at the right time.' It is signed 'Pepina'. What do you make of it? It sounds rather like a threat."

"What do *you* make of it, mother?" said Lucy.

"Why, the question is, who the traitor was to whom Philip was to give the message?"

"Well, you know who was with him."

"Yes. I suppose you are right. As usual, a woman in the case. It looks like some disgraceful intrigue. The writing is that of a peasant woman. I wonder who poor Pepina was."

"I think," said Lucy, "this really does throw some light on the change in Philip's manner to Sir Edward."

"Very likely," said her mother. "He must have behaved badly to the girl, and Philip disapproved. I suppose we shall never know anything more about it. Some sad story, only too common a one, I am sorry to say."

At this moment the servant opened the door and announced Sir Edward Wilson.

For some days after his return to town, Wilson had felt unable to renew his relations with the Cranstons. It was horrible to think of seeing them again. That he should write a letter of condolence was inevitable, considering their former intimacy.

It would naturally be expected of him, and its omission might awake suspicion; but to write it cost him an agonising effort. The situation was appalling; to think of their reading expressions of sympathy written by the hand that had done the deed! But it had to be done, and he got through it somehow, though the letters seemed to him to be written in blood. And he pictured to himself Lucy reading it. If she only knew! It was dreadful to think of. She had attracted him as no other woman had ever done. In his selfish way he really loved her; he thought she was worthy to share his fortunes and would take her place with dignity and grace as his wife in the high position to which he aspired.

But now, that, he thought, must all be at an end; he must think of her no more. To ask the hand of the sister of the man he had killed was too horrible to contemplate. Another trouble presented itself. He must meet Philip's mother and sister as soon as a decent time had elapsed since the funeral; he had been a constant visitor at the house, and to drop at once all intimacy would be dangerous. He would have to face them, but God alone knew how he could do it. How could he show his guilty face again in that familiar room associated with recollections of pleasant meetings and innocent intercourse?

But time went on. The murder was forgotten, no suspicion was ever directed against him, law and politics combined to absorb his attention more and more, and the first hest of his self-reproach and remorse began to cool. He even succeeded in finding excuses for himself after all, Cranston had struck the first blow; he only acted in self-defence, and the quarrel ended unfortunately for poor Cranston, for whom he sincerely grieved. And then Pepina. He had almost forgotten that part of the business. Poor Pepina; it was so very sad, but how could he have foreseen that she would take the matter so seriously. Those Italians were so very excitable. Still he blamed himself for not having provided somehow for her future. However, there was no help for that now.

He determined at last that the time had come when he must go and see the Cranstons, or his absence might be remarked upon. And now he did not somehow feel the same reluctance as at first. Having satisfied or rather blunted his own conscience, he had a feeling that what had been enough for himself might satisfy others as well, and that as he had brought himself to believe that he was rather the victim of circumstances in which by accident he had to his great regret injured others, the same view would be taken by the world at large should the matter ever come to light.

He called then, as we have seen, on Mrs. Cranston, and managed to impress her with his sympathy. He was quieter and more subdued than usual, and Mrs. Cranston approved his manner, which seemed to show real feeling. Lucy, as we know, was not present, which was a disappointment, for he had looked forward to seeing her. If she could not now be his, still it would be pleasant to be with her again on something like the old friendly relations. Mrs. Cranston thought him improved; less masterful and self-assertive, and she was touched by his kindly words and manner.

He thought a good deal of Lucy as he walked away. To give her up cost him a pang. Every memory of her graceful ways, her bright intelligence, and her ready sympathy made it more difficult. After all, was it out of the question, he said to himself, that she should be his wife? And then the thought rushed upon him, "Suppose she found me out after we were married?"

That was horrible; too horrible. But was it at all possible that this should happen? The whole thing was sunk into oblivion, and unlikely ever to be heard of again. There could be no danger.

"I am sure," said he to himself, "I could make her a happy woman. I can offer her position, wealth, and influence; Lucy would make a *grande dame* of whom I should be proud."

It was then with a determination to persist in the course, to prevent which her brother had fallen by his hand, that Sir Edward Wilson knocked at the door a fortnight later, and asked whether Mrs. Cranston was at home. He was shown into the drawing-room, and there, as we know, he found Lucy as well as her mother.

They rose to meet him, Mrs. Cranston laying on the table the mysterious paper which Lucy had given her to read. They thought Sir Edward looking worn and aged, and he explained rather hurriedly that he had had a good deal to worry him of late. They talked of politics, and of a great speech he had made in the House which had been much praised, and he was pleased to hear that Lucy had read it in *The Times* and admired it. He talked well, and they were pleased with his manner, which was a good deal softened from its former style. He bore the inevitable allusions to poor Philip with more composure than he could have anticipated, and replied to their questions that no further clue had been found as to the author of the crime.

"For my part," said Mrs. Cranston, "I wish they would drop the inquiry, and let the whole affair be forgotten."

"So do I," said Lucy, "and so I am sure would poor Philip if he could speak. I am quite willing to leave the murderer to the torments of his own conscience."

Sir Edward said nothing, and soon after rose to take his leave. As he shook hands with Mrs. Cranston he was standing by the table, and his eye fell on the paper Mrs. Cranston had laid down as he entered the room. She felt him start; he dropped her hand, and, as she looked at him in surprise she saw he had turned ashy pale. He staggered for a moment and supported himself by the table, before recovering himself.

To her expression of fear that he was not well, he explained rather incoherently that he felt a little dizzy for the moment; that he had been overworking himself, and supposed his doctor was right in telling him he wanted him a rest. But he could not recover his wonted composure as he bowed himself out of the room, declining Mrs. Cranston's invitation to sit down and wait till he felt better. Lucy stood aloof, and avoiding shaking hands with him, dismissed him with a bow.

"There, mother," said she when the door closed, "you see we were right. If ever a guilty conscience could show itself it did so now. Depend upon it there is some tragedy connected with poor Pepina."

"It certainly was very odd," said her mother. "I thought he would have fainted. Are you sure it was the sight of that paper that upset him?"

"Quite sure. I saw his eye fall upon it; and I saw him read it, and then he changed colour at once, and staggered as if he would have fallen. Nobody but a man of his great self-command could have recovered himself as he did in a minute."

"I think, my dear," said Mrs. Cranston, "that paper should be taken care of. It is possible it may be wanted some day."

"I think so too. I will take it to my room and lock it up." Said Lucy.

As Wilson walked away his head was in a whirl. He called a cab and went home, and shut himself up in his study. All the edifice of self-deception, exculpation, and complacency which he had built up around him had fallen to the ground at the sight of that fatal paper of which Philip told him before he died. He was left naked and exposed to all the tortures of an awakened conscience. He saw Cranston lying in his blood, Pepina in her watery grave, and himself their murderer. Where now were his shallow evasions; where were the vain pretences with which he had deceived himself.

He saw himself as he was, a criminal, a double criminal, with blood on his hands of one who had loved him, and one who had been his trusted friend. It was too much; why not end it all with a dose or a pistol shot? Then at all events the secret would die with him, his fair fame would be saved, and it would never be known that the great lawyer, the brilliant politician should by right have been standing in the dock at the Old Bailey.

And that paper: *ti rivedro all' ora giusta.* When am I to see her again, and why would she come? In his present dejected state he never doubted that she would make her word good. A cold shudder ran through his frame. He was to see her again, but when and where! Philip's last words were "I leave you to Pepina." Pepina was to avenge them both. Well, let her come, things could not be worse than they were. He wished he were dead and all were over.

Another year had slipped away, and Lucy and her mother were sitting as we last saw them in their pleasant room looking at the spring blossoms that were bursting in the garden of the Square. Lucy was engaged to be married shortly to Frederick Warren, a young barrister, rising into good practice, who had been a friend of her brother Philip, and was with him on that fatal circuit. He was one of the last to see him before he went on his last walk, and he had attended the inquest, which he thought very badly managed and too easily satisfied. Mrs. Cranston and Lucy were now expecting him to drop in to tea, as he usually did when his day's work was done. He came in radiant, for the case in which he was engaged under one of the big-wigs of the bar had won the day, though the great Attorney-general had been opposed to them.

"I think he was rather sick about it, Lucy," said he, "for he cannot bear to be beaten. There never was a man more determined to have his own way in everything."

"Lucy says he is an idolater, and that the idol he worships is himself," said Mrs. Cranston.

"A very good description," said Warren. "He is an egoist, if ever there was one. I doubt if he would let anything stand between him and his pleasure if he could help it; and yet at the bottom there is something good about him which comes out so long as you don't thwart him."

"He is a very masterful person," said Lucy, "and I think he would have made a very good tyrant in the Middle Ages, like Sigismondo Malatesta, and Bernabo Visconti, and the rest of the Italian despots."

"By the way," said Warren, "that reminds me of your story about him and an Italian girl. Some paper you found that you showed him, and it upset him a good deal."

"Of course we know nothing about it," said Mrs. Cranston, "but I fancy there is some tragedy in the case, and that Sir Edward was implicated in it, and to blame for it."

"Do you know," said Lucy, "I have been having some curious

dreams about it, which made me rather uncomfortable, especially as they were followed by a reality. But you don't believe in dreams, Frederick, and you will laugh at me if I tell you."

"Certainly not," said he, "especially since they have made you uncomfortable, and still more wonderful, were followed by a reality."

"There now," said she, "you are laughing at me already."

"No. I'll promise to be serious indeed," said he.

"Well then," said Lucy "you will remember the girl's name was Pepina and she was an Italian, and to judge by her writing a peasant woman. My dream was rather vague, but it has been repeated three times. I seemed to be in a vineyard; there were many figures there but all very indistinct, except one face which showed up clearly, a beautiful face, quite classical, like a Greek statue. I could not see what she was doing, for the whole scene was misty, only the face was clear; and then all seemed to fade away and change to a riverside.

"It was nearly dark, but I saw something in the water, something white, and as I looked I saw it was the same beautiful face looking up at me out of the water. It troubled me a good deal and I awoke. But the dream was repeated twice more, just the same and no more of it. Do you think it was Pepina?"

"I think you had Pepina in your mind when you went to bed, and invented the pictures in your sleep."

"Well, but why three times? And I never thought of the river and poor Pepina in it. That at all events was no invention of mine. I think she drowned herself and that was the tragedy, and that the dream was sent to let me know."

"Well, perhaps so. But what of the reality that followed?"

"If you don't believe in dreams," said Lucy, "I suppose you won't believe in ghosts."

"Nay, I don't say that," said Frederick. "But what have you to say about ghosts?"

"Well, just this. Yesterday, as I was crossing the park to come home, I saw the same face as that in my dream."

"Indeed," said Frederick, "that is curious. What happened?"

"Nothing happened. It was getting dusk and I was rather late, when I saw a woman in black standing where I should pass her. As I came up, she turned and looked at me. It was the same lovely classical face that I had seen in my dream. I should know it again anywhere. It was very pale and sad. She said nothing but looked hard at me, and I was so frightened that I dared not speak to her. I heard footsteps approaching and looked round, and when I turned again she was gone."

"Didn't you see her figure moving away?"

"No. She had vanished utterly."

"That is a very curious story," said both of her listeners—and they sat for a few minutes in silence.

"Then you think," said Warren, "that poor Pepina, for I assume, of course, you dreamt of her. Wishes to establish some communication with you."

"I do indeed, and I fancy it concerns Sir Edward Wilson."

"You know, Lucy," said he, "I am, or rather have been a confirmed disbeliever in ghosts and spiritualism, but I am not such a prig as to believe myself infallible. You experience is certainly very strange. I wonder whether anything more will come of it. I think you should write it all down at the time so as to be sure of the facts. They often get exaggerated by repetition of the story."

"There is another thing, however, that it occurs to me. Do you remember what was on the paper that so upset Sir Edward?"

"No. I forget," said Warren.

"It said, 'I shall see you again at the right time.' Now do you think this figure has come to show itself to him?"

"Who knows. If we can guess the story right, Sir Edward betrayed poor Pepina and deserted her, and she went and drowned herself. But, of course, we have no proof of anything of the kind, except your dream and vision, and that, as we lawyers say, is not evidence."

"No, that is true. But I don't envy him his feelings if he visited by his victim. It should be enough to make a man mad. Perhaps this is the right time—'*l'ora giusta,*' of the letter."

"But why should she come to you of all people in the world?"

"I think it is because I am Philip's sister, and it was to him her note was written, and I have the note itself in my keeping."

"And have you seen much of Sir Edward lately?"

"No, very little," said Mrs. Cranston. "I fancy he does not like the recollection of having, in a manner, betrayed himself when he saw that paper. He only comes now when he is pretty sure of finding company here."

"I'm glad of that," said Warren, who remembered the time when it was thought Sir Edward and Lucy were to make a match of it."

London was at the height of the season. Fashion and society were in full swing, Parliament was sitting and many measures of consequence were under debate. Sir Edward Wilson was conspicuous among the champions of the Government: never had he carried more weight in the councils of the nation, never had he shone more brilliantly in debate, never had he been so formidable to his opponents. It was thought the Chancellor wished to retire, and by common consent Sir Edward was regarded as the next custodian of the Great Seal.

He had dropped in one evening at Athenæum for a cup of tea before going down to the House, and as he stood talking and laughing amid a group of friends who were congratulating him on the part he had played in his last night's debate, he felt he had touched the zenith of his fortune and that the great prize of his profession was almost within his grasp. When his friends left him he sat down to his tea and idly took up an evening paper that someone had left on the chair at his side. As he glanced over it, his eye fell on a paragraph that made his heart stand still.

### The Northborough Murder

It will be remembered that about two years ago a shocking murder was committed near Northborough, the author of which has till now escaped justice. The victim was Mr. Philip Cranston, a rising barrister, who was attending circuit in that town. The body was found stripped of all articles of value and hidden on a thick part of the wood. Hitherto the police have had no clue to lead them to the discovery of the criminal. Yesterday, however, the arrest was made of a man of bad character, in whose possession some of the property taken from the unfortunate gentleman was found. The capture reflects great credit on the local police, and illustrates the old saying that *murder will out*. The man is named Abel Sanders, and we understand he will be brought before the magistrates on Tuesday.

The blow for the moment stunned him. This was an eventuality on which he had not counted. He saw at once how it affected him. This wretched yokel would be tried for his life, and might be convicted and hanged. He himself, and no other, could save the poor wretch, but he could only do it at his own expense, by changing places with the prisoner. Had it come at last to this? He turned the matter over this way and that, but saw no escape from the dilemma, if the man were convicted. It was of course, possible that he would be acquitted, and if so all would be well. At all events he would wait and see the result of the inquiry before the magistrates, and then decide what must be done.

When he got home he found as expected, a subpoena requiring him to appear as a witness before the bench of magistrates at Northborough. The evidence at the inquest had been read over and his presence was necessary, he having been the last person in poor Philip's company.

He found the court crowded, for the arrest had made a great stir in the county. There was a large attendance of the county magistrates on the bench, some of whom were known to him and greeted him as a distinguished friend. Among the witnesses he was surprised to see Lucy Cranston, who had been summoned to swear to the property of her brother. Warren had come with her to see her through this disagreeable business, for which he thought, as did poor Lucy, a servant would have done as well. Sir Edward had heard of their engagement, but it distressed him less than it would have done twelve months before. He had long given up any pretensions in that quarter.

The prisoner was brought in, a shambling, ne'er-do-well sort of yokel, who stared stupidly about him, and did not seem to realise the seriousness of his position. The evidence was much the same as at the inquest, with the addition of the new matter connected with the arrest. The watch and chain, and various small articles that were found in the prisoner's possession were identified by Lucy as having belonged to her brother. The policeman who found the body told his tale over again, and Sir Edward repeated the evidence he had given before the coroner.

One of the magistrates, however, who had known Cranston, asked a question which caused some surprise in court.

"I believe, Sir Edward, if I am right, there had been some sort of quarrel between you and Mr. Cranston?"

"There certainly was at one time," replied Sir Edward, "a slight coolness on Mr. Cranston's part towards me, arising from a trifling family matter, but I am happy to think that that had passed and we were good friends again. In fact it was Mr. Cranston who proposed our going for a walk together on that fatal day."

This was confirmed by other witnesses who had been present and heard Cranston give the invitation, and nothing further was said. But Warren looked at Lucy and raised his eyebrows.

The prisoner's story was that he found the dead body in the wood, and he admitted taking from it the things found in his possession. He said also:

"I see two gents a walking into the wood, and after a bit only one of 'em come out. If you can spot that man I warrant he'll be the one as you want."

Asked if he could identify the man he saw come out of the wood he said. "No, he was too far off. It was a biggish man, something the size of the gen'lman a setting there," and he pointed to Sir Edward.

Sir Edward rose at once and said he had no doubt the man was speaking the truth. "Your worship will remember I said in my evidence that my poor friend Cranston and I entered the wood together, and that we parted, he continued his walk further on, and I returning alone. I have no doubt it was I whom the prisoner saw leaving the wood."

There was no more evidence forthcoming, and the Justices, after conferring together, agreed that it was a case for further investigation, and the man was committed for trial at the forthcoming assizes on two counts, one of wilful murder, and the other of unlawful possession of the property found on him.

As they were leaving the court with the crowd that was pouring out, Lucy clutched Warren's arm.

"Look, look," said she.

He followed her gaze and just caught sight of a pale face, beautiful and sad, turned towards then for a moment, and then the figure was lost in the crowd. They sought to find her but in vain.

"It is she again," said Lucy. "Now you will know her. This cannot be the last time we shall see her. Depend on it she is not here for nothing."

Wilson's reflections as he went back to town were not agreeable. The man was not acquitted as he had hoped, and he did not like the question put to him by Mr. Turner from the bench. It might direct suspicion on him. Mr. Turner had, no doubt, been talking to his friends about the case, and may have made uncomfortable suggestions, which would be remembered when the matter came on for trial. As on the former occasion before the magisterial examination, he comforted himself by the thought that the trial might end in an acquittal, and that the whole matter would then sink again into the oblivion from which the arrest of Abel Sanders had lifted it.

But on the other hand the man might be convicted and sentenced to death. What was he to do then? It rested with him and him alone to rescue an innocent man from the gallows, but at what a price! Could he afford to pay it? He was no coward. It was not the fear of punishment that weighed on him. But the shame, the disgrace of being dragged down from his splendid position to ignominy. He had so much to lose.

Wilson, though arbitrary and self-seeking, was not an entirely unscrupulous man. Self interest at times had driven him towards what he naturally disapproved, but he now felt there was a limit beyond which he could go. Brought face to face with this tremendous problem, he felt that truth and justice left him no choice, and that there was nothing before him bur ruin.

However, there was still the chance of the trial ending in an acquittal, and that would solve all his difficulties.

It was in the hopeful state of mind created by this last consideration that he entered his chambers in the temple one morning a short time after the Northborough inquiry, and asked his clerk what had come in since yesterday.

The clerk ran through a list of matters, small and great, which had to be attended to, and then produced an official letter that had just been handed in.

"A brief for you, sir, from the Crown, for the prosecution, in the case of *Rex. v.* Abel Sanders. I think that was the murder down at Northborough. You will remember, sir, you had to attend the inquest. With you will be, let me see, Mr. Jones and Mr. Evans."

Sir Edward sank into his chair and said nothing. He dismissed his clerk and said he would call him when he wanted him later. For the moment the monstrous situation paralysed him. He felt that to hold his peace during the trial was bad enough, but it was impossible for him to stand up and prosecute an innocent man for the crime he himself had committed. He could not think of it without horror: at all events he must escape from that position, and he would, of course, decline the brief.

He wrote to that effect to the Hone Secretary, returning the brief on the plea that his other engagements and his Parliamentary work, which just then was very arduous, obliged him, to his regret, to decline to act. He observed also that he had appeared as a witness in the case and might be called again.

The Secretary, however,, was persistent. He said the matter was very important as complaints had come from that district of insufficient protection against the frequent robberies with violence that had been committed: that hitherto no criminals had been captured, and that should it prove that Abel Sanders was guilty the example of his punishment would be useful. For that reason it had been decided to employ the best talent at the Bar, and to brief the Attorney-General.

Undaunted by this Sir Edward went to see the official, who received him rather coldly, and made light of the objection he raised on the ground that he had been called as a witness before the magistrates.

"Your evidence was not important, Sir Edward, and we can do without calling you at the trial very well."

As Sir Edward persisted, the secretary said in some surprise, and with a little irritation, he could not see the difficulty.

"I do not understand what motive you can possibly have for declining, Sir Edward," said he.

The word motive alarmed Sir Edward. It must not be supposed he had any motive beyond the difficulties he had mentioned. He hastened to plead again pressure of work as his reason.

The great man at once recovered his good temper.

"We all know the demand the public interest makes on Sir Edward's time," he said, smiling. "But this is a very simple case. The man is an old offender, and the property was found on him. It will not give you much trouble. So I conclude you will act, and am much obliged to you. Good day."

And then, shaking hands, he accompanied him to the door and dismissed him. The week before the trial was spent by Sir Edward in a sort of ghastly dream. He lived, as it were, in hell, for hell itself could not be worse. Some deadly diabolical web seemed to him to enveloping him and dragging him ever lower and lower into an abyss of crime. He could trace a horrible sequence in all that had befallen him; crime grew out of crime the whole had hung together; he had been drawn step by step along the same dark path which was leading him to perdition.

Till that fatal Italian tour his life had been clean and honourable. The tragedy of Pepina began it, and then the devil's toils began to close around him. Pepina's death led to the second tragedy, that fatal murderous blow in the forest at Northborough. And as if the devil had not got him already involved in his meshes, he was now forcing him to a worse sin still, to drag an innocent man to the gallows in order to conceal his own crime and save himself from shame and punishment.

"Worse, far worse this," he said "than the former crimes. Whatever palliation there might have been for them, this was deliberate murder."

For his victim, indeed, he felt no pity. He hated Abel Sanders with a bitter hatred as the author of his present misery. Why could not the scoundrel have hid his spoils better? He compared his own brilliant position with that of this ignorant clown. "What," he thought, "is that ignoble life worth in comparison with mine? What is the fairness of putting it in the balance against one of so much more in value? The wretch was a mean thief; he bore a bad character, and had been in prison more than once. He would probably have come to the gallows anyhow, whereas I, whose life and honour he puts in jeopardy, can ill be spared. And yet," thought he, "a third death will lie at my door! My God! What have I done to bring all this upon me?"

He was not convinced by his own excuses. His self-respect was gone; he knew he was sinking lower and lower into the abyss of guilt; that the toils sun about him by some devilish agency were dragging him down to perdition; but he had no power to resist. A fatal necessity was upon him, a spell enveloped him. And he knew that whatever happened he must now go through with this accursed business.

It was remarked, as the day of trial grew near, that he became haggard and depressed. His erect frame began to stoop, his step was languid and his eyes dull.

"Wilson is killing himself with overwork," said his friends. "If he does not look out, and take things more easily, he will not reach the Woolsack after all."

The court was crowded to suffocation on the day of the trial.

All the count magnates attended, and several members of the circuit had been there at the time of Philip Cranston's disappearance two years before. The Lord Chief Justice was to preside, and it was known that the Attorney-General had been briefed for the prosecution. Among the members of the Bar who were present was Frederick Warren, who had promised to bring a report of the trial to Mrs. Cranston and Lucy. Their interest in the trial was not great, and they rather wished to know nothing about it. But Warren thought it necessary on their account to be present and take notes of what occurred.

It was late when he returned and sat down with them, and they could see by his manner that something unusual had happened. He was much agitated, and it was some minutes before he began his story.

"I've strange things to tell you," he said at last, "and I don't quite know myself what to make of it all. It is mostly about Wilson, and the trial is not finished yet. When he came into court I hardly knew him. You never saw a man so changed. His face was yellow, his lips dry and parched, his cheeks were sunk in, and he looked more dead than alive. Everyone was shocked, even the judge, who sent a message to ask whether Sir Edward was unwell. However, the trial began; the jury were sworn, and witnesses were called and examined, but it was all pretty much the same as when you and I were at the magistrate's court a month ago, Lucy.

"I need not bother you with all that all over again. When Wilson got up the excitement became greater. Everybody was anxious to hear the great Attorney-General, whose reputation as a speaker and debater stood so high. I was pretty near him, and watched him closely. He spoke well, but I did not like the tone of his speech. He seemed inspired with a sort of venomous spite against the poor devil of a wretch in the dock, very different from his usual generous way of dealing with the evidence rather than the criminal I think it made the judge himself rather uncomfortable, for several times he was on the pint of interposing a remark, but apparently altered his mind.

"I think, however, Wilson did himself harm with the jury, who, as all honest Englishmen do, like fair play, and don't like to see a man hit when he is down. This went on for some time, and I could see from looks that passed among us barristers that Wilson's speech was making a bad impression. Still he was speaking brilliantly and well, when an awful thing happened. He suddenly faltered and put his hand to his head. I looked up at him and saw him turn ashy pale, with his eyes fixed on a figure that had risen from the well of the court just in front of him. It was the figure of a woman in black, who looked him full in the face. She was not a yard from him.

"It was all a matter of less than a minute, and then with a sort of sobbing gasp, Wilson covered his face with his hands. "At last you are come," he said, and then sank on his seat. There was a great commotion; ushers ran and brought him water. Everyone was standing up, even the judge was leaning over his desk. Every eye was on Sir Edward, but I looked at the woman as she passed me to go out. She was close to me, and I saw her face, that beautiful sad face which you showed me at Northborough. Inquiry was made for her, but she had disappeared during the confusion, and no trace of her could be found. The ushers declared the doors were locked and no one had left the court since the trial began, to their certain knowledge. Now, what do you think of that?"

"I think," said Lucy, "the right hour, *l'ora giusta*, had struck, and she saw him again as she had promised."

"But what happened afterwards?" said Mrs. Cranston.

"Well, of course the trial was suspended, the prisoner was removed, and the court broke up in some confusion. Sir Edward, in a semiconscious state, was carried back to his hotel, where all sorts of inquiries were made after him, and then I came away to tell you all about it, just catching my train as it were on the point of starting."

"It is all so strange," said Mrs. Cranston, "that I don't know what to think. Is the trial to go on tomorrow?"

"I hardly know. The situation is so unusual. They may put it off till the next assizes. But it all depends on Sir Edward."

"Do you think the poor man is guilty?" asked Lucy.

The question seemed to disturb Warren, and he did not answer for some time. At last he said: "Well, to tell the truth, I don't. But I have ideas about it that I hardly like to put into words. It is too serious a matter to speak of lightly, and I have little ground to go upon."

Wilson was lying on a sofa in his room at the Bull's Head. The doctor had seen him and given him a sedative, and advised perfect rest and quiet. He was much shaken, and gladly acquiesced in the doctor's prescription, refusing to see any of the friends who came to inquire after him.

So he had seen Pepina at last. She had come as she promised, and it was at the right time that she came, for it was just in time to save him from a ghastly crime that now, in his weak and nervous state, seemed to show itself nakedly in all its enormity. He had been about to declare himself a convicted believer in the guilt of the wretch in the dock, whom he knew to be innocent, while he himself was the real culprit. His conscience awoke. He knew himself to have sunk to a level of infamy which he felt would make men recoil from him in disgust were the truth known.

It had come to that. He, the envied leader of his profession, the brilliant politician, who had the world at his feet, was in reality a sordid wretch of whose meanness and treachery Abel Sanders would have been ashamed. From the worst consequences of his guilt Pepina had come to save him. She had come not as the avenger, but as his good angel; not in anger, but in mercy. His heart went out to her in love and gratitude. In the gathering dusk he seemed to see her again before him. It was the face he had loved that was looking at him, sadly but not unkindly. The face that had been bright and happy till he came to blast her innocence and then betray her and leave her.

"Pepina," he cried, "do you forgive me, for I cannot forgive myself? You have saved me from another crime. I am not worthy of your forgiveness."

He seemed to feel her near him, to feel her breath on his face, her touch on his hands, and then he knew he was forgiven, and sank into a quiet slumber.

All England was startled next morning by a heading in large capitals on the newspaper posters—

SUDDEN DEATH OF THE ATTORNEY-GENERAL

The report ran thus:

We regret to announce the sudden death of Sir Edward Wilson, K.C., Attorney-General. The learned gentleman had apparently been ailing for some little time owing, in the opinion of his friends, to overwork. His appearance in court yesterday at Northborough caused general concern, which was changed to consternation when he suddenly broke down in his speech and had to be carried to his rooms in the Bull's Head Hotel. His condition when the doctors left him last night did not appear critical, but we regret to say the learned gentleman was found dead in his bed early this morning. He had apparently died in his sleep.

In another part of the paper was a long obituary notice of his career and distinctions.

When the court met that morning nothing was talked of but the death of their great chief. The head of the Bar made a moving speech about the loss of their eminent and distinguished colleague, which was listened to by his audience, all standing. The judge followed with a few remarks, and was much affected, and it was some time before they proceeded to the business of the day. When the case of *Rex v.* Abel Sanders was called up, his lordship asked the junior counsel for the prosecution whether they were prepared to go on with the case, or whether, under these unhappy circumstances, they would prefer to let it stand over.

But before they could answer, a letter was put in his hands by a messenger from the Bull's Head. It was in Sir Edward's writing, and the judge, after reading a few lines, changed countenance and retired to his private room. The counsel, both of the prosecution and defence, were shortly afterwards called to join him, and the letter was laid before them. The contents were never published, but it was understood by the few who were better informed that it contained a full and true account of the death of Philip Cranston, written by Sir Edward Wilson the evening before he died.

When they returned to court the judge asked, as he had done before, whether the remaining counsellors for the prosecution were prepared to go on with the case, and the senior of the two, Mr. Jones, rose and said that from instructions he had received he withdrew the charge on the first count, and was prepared to proceed with that on the second count only.

As the prisoner had confessed his guilt on this count, he was sentenced to a short imprisonment, and so ended the case.

Some years afterwards Lucy talked to her husband about the trial, and asked him what he thought was the real history of its sudden collapse after Sir Edward's death, which had always puzzled her.

"Do you remember, Lucy, at the magistrates' examination, a question being asked by Mr. Turner, one of the magistrates, who had been a friend of poor Philips?"

"Yes. He asked whether there had not been a quarrel between Sir Edward and Philip. But you surely don't mean—"

"Well," said Frederick, "let us leave it there. *De mortuis nil nisi bonum*—we have need to pray *lead us not into temptation*."

# The Red House

On the edge of a great common, not many miles from London, there still stands an ancient red brick house with many gables, dating from the time of James I. Two wings of a later date have been added, but they do not interfere with the parent block. Standing originally as the principal house of a country village, it is now surrounded by modern villas, from which it courts seclusion within its high walls and gates, and the shady old-fashioned garden, into which, in summer at all events, the prying eyes of neighbours cannot penetrate.

It seems to stand aloof from its modern surroundings, as a gentleman of the old school might shrink from the slang and vulgarity of the smart set of today. Within are stately rooms, loftier than usual for the date, some with old chimney-pieces and rich fretted plaster ceilings, in one of which appears the arms of the prosperous East Indian merchant who built the house when Shakespeare was still alive and Milton unborn. At the time of our story, however, it was still a country place. Here and there round the village green were a few comfortable houses where well-to-do London merchants sought repose after the turmoil of the City, and within a short mile was the stately home of the Lord of the manor, with its wide-spread park stretching away towards London, and its great lake in the valley below the garden terraces.

In the reign of George III. this was the home of Sir Richard Hetherington, baronet and Justice of the Peace, who was connected with the great family at the Manor House, and had considerable property also in Kent near Sevenoaks. He had ridden down in the afternoon from his town house in Queen's Square, Westminster, and was reading a note put into his hands just as he was starting:

Mr. Dawes to Sir Richard sends compliments begs pardon for not meeting him at the Bedford according to appointment. Did not dine till five and in such company as pushed the bottle about, marvellously quick that about 7 o'clock his humble servant was very unfit for St. James's. Sunday Warwick Court.
To
Sir Richard Hetherington
Queen's Square.

"Dicky Dawes," said he to his wife laughing, "is a bit too fond of the bottle, but is a good fellow at bottom. You know, my dear, he comes here tomorrow."

"I like Mr. Dawes well enough," said she, "when he is not in his cups."

"A plague rich fellow, Dawes, so they say," said William Hetherington, Sir Richard's nephew, who was in the room and listening to the conversation.

"Aye, he is well enough to do," said Sir Richard, who did not like the tone of the remark, "but what is that to you, William?"

"To me, uncle? Why nothing at all. How do you suppose he will get here?"

"On horseback, I suppose, over the bridge and by the common. I have warned him not to ride late, for there are highwaymen about."

"Jerry Abershaw," said Lady Hetherington. "They say he is here again and has stopped the coach on the High Road."

"Oh! Jerry Abershaw!" said William, rather rudely. "Jerry Abershaw would have to be in a dozen places at once, if we were to believe all people say of him. Mr. Dawes will be safe enough on his ride, and there is no need to frighten him."

And so saying, William Hetherington swung out of the

room.

"A young cub!" said Sir Richard, as the door closed behind him. "He grows more insufferable every day."

"I wish he would go away and do something for himself," said his wife.

"So do I, my dear, heartily. But my poor brother has left him in my charge, and as his guardian I must see him through his minority. However, in a few months he will be of age, and then our troubles will be over."

"But what will he do with himself when he is his own master? I fear he will go from bad to worse."

"I fear so too, but I see no way to do more for him than I have done," said Sir Richard. "He will have a decent patrimony if he does not fool it away when he has it, after he comes of age. I have nursed it carefully for him during his minority. But from hints that have been given me, I fear he has got into bad company. I am glad my poor brother is not here to see it."

William Hetherington was a likely-looking lad, well-built and not ill-favoured, though there was a shifty glance of his eye, and a weak expression of the mouth, that were not encouraging. Losing his father early in life, he had been brought up by his uncle; but he learned little at school, and profited less by the severe discipline of those days. And when the time came for settling him in life, every attempt to establish him in any useful calling had been unsuccessful.

Mr. Richard Dawes, the expected visitor, was a middle-aged gentleman of moderate fortune, and a small estate in Kent near Sir Richard's property in that county. He was a jovial, easy going man, fond of good living and good company, and very popular among his friends and acquaintances. If he sometimes overdid it, as on the occasion mentioned in his letter to Sir Richard, he generally managed to carry his liquor as well as any man living in that hard-drinking age, and seldom fuddled his wits with the fumes of his potations. He had a strong vein of native shrewdness in his composition, and a dry caustic humour that never failed him in an emergency; and nobody ever tried to score off him without coming out of the encounter badly.

But when Mr. Dawes arrived in the evening of the day following that when the discussion we have reported between Sir Richard and his lady took place, his usual quiet humour was sadly upset. As he dismounted at the door, and gave his nag to the stableman, he was full of grunts and muttered growls, and when he shook hands with his host and hostess, his flushed face and perturbed expression made them both ask what was the matter.

"The matter!" quoth Mr. Dawes "The matter is this, Sir Richard, that two rogues have waylaid me on your confounded common, and damme if they haven't robbed me of my purse, my watch, and whatever else they took a fancy to in my valise. What do you think of that my lady?"

They both exclaimed together that it was abominable, and that information should be sent at once to the magistrates, and men be set on the offenders' track.

"Much good will that do me," growled poor Mr. Dawes. "They may catch the thieves and hang them, but that won't give me my property back."

"And should you know the men again if you saw them?" asked my lady, while Sir Richard was gone to send messengers off at once to give the alarm.

"They were both masked," replied he; "both were young men, the slighter of the two a mere lad, I fancy. I think I might know their voices if I heard them, for they were talking to one another while they rifled my unhappy valise."

"And whereabouts did it happen?"

"About a mile from this house," said Mr. Dawes, just where a cart-track turns off from the bridle-path to go a windmill that stands in the waste. And when they had done they galloped off that way. The younger man guarded me with a pistol at my head, while the other plundered the valise that was strapped on the saddle."

"How dreadful," said Lady Hetherington. "But it is well you came off with your life."

"I suppose, after all," said Mr. Dawes, "it is as well I was un-armed, for otherwise I could not have helped giving the rascals a shot, and then getting two back myself, for they were two to one, though one of them seemed only a lad."

"I suppose they knew you had no arms," said lady Hether-ington.

"I am not sure of that," said he, "for the younger man, as they galloped up and stopped me, cried, 'hands up,' and with his con-founded pistol at my head, I had to obey."

"They say Jerry Abershaw is at work here again," said my lady. "I doubt he was one of the two, but who could the other one be; a mere lad you say?"

"Ay, ay, Jerry may have been the elder man very likely," said Mr. Dawes, "for they managed it cleverly enough, and he is a practised hand, As for the youngster, the sooner he comes to the gallows the better, for he has taken to the trade betimes, and should be scotched before he does more mischief."

"Yes, I suppose so," said my lady, "and yet it is sad to think of one so young coming to such an end."

They were at supper when William, Sir Richard's nephew came in. He had been riding, and said he had been over to the town to get his whip mended, and that made him late home.

Mr. Dawes had seen him before and did not like him, for he thought him ill-mannered and empty-headed, and wondered how Sir Richard and his lady could put up with his idle ways.

They supped in the hall, and then adjourned to the great chamber above, with its fine plaster ceiling and walls hung with tapestry, for it was Sir Richard's fancy to keep the old place unaltered as it had come to him, in the mode of the preceding century, before the invasion of continental fashions from France and Holland.

The sun shone next morning, and after breakfast they saun-tered about the garden. Like the house itself, the garden, which lay behind it, was kept in the style in which it had been laid out by Robert Bell, the founder in the days of James I. There were the straight paths and formal parterres where Mrs. Alice Bell used to grow her gilliflowers and roses, divided by miniature hedges of box or privet; there was the sun-dial with its motto:

*As these hours doth passe away*
*So doth the life of men decay,*

And beyond the spacious grass-plot was the raised terrace walk with seats overlooking the meadows, where were the cows.

Lady Hetherington observed with some surprise the pleasure Mr. Dawes seemed to take in her nephew William's company. Putting his arm through that of the seemingly unwilling lad, Mr. Dawes tried to get him to talk, William, awkward and embarrassed, tried to escape, and only answered in monosyllables or short sentences to Mr. Dawes's flow of conversation. He was giving William a full account of the disaster of the day before, and describing the persons of the two robbers as minutely as he could. But the story, far from interesting William, seemed to cause him much uneasiness. At last he was released, and, when he was out of earshot, Mr. Dawes, smiling to himself, muttered, "Very like. Very like. I think it will do."

From the flower garden they wandered into the kitchen gardens, where the fruit was ripening on the walls of mellow red brick. There were some tempting plums just out of reach of Lady Hetherington, and she called William to get them for her. He had both his arms stretched above his head when a loud voice behind exclaimed, "Hands up! As that young villain said yesterday." William spun round, as pale as ashes, and faced Mr. Dawes, who was looking at him with a sarcastic smile.

"Why, William," said his aunt, "what's the matter? You look as if you have seen a ghost."

"Perhaps he has, my lady," said Dawes, with a short laugh, as he turned away, and followed Sir Richard to another part of the garden. "I think he was pretty nigh making one yesterday," he continued to himself, "What is to be done now? Poor Sir Richard! He ought to know; but how am I ever to tell him?"

"What did Mr. Dawes mean William?" asked his aunt, when

Mr. Dawes was out of hearing.

"Some of his nonsense," said William. "He is always saying disagreeable things to me. I hate him."

But William was sadly discomposed, and had a scared look that Lady Hetherington could not help noticing.

They dined at the fashionable hour of five, and both Sir Richard and his lady could not help wondering at the unaccountable predilection Mr. Dawes showed for William's society and conversation. He placed himself by his side and plied him with questions, to which he only got short and sulky answers.

"We have spread the news of the robbery far and near," said Sir Richard, "but have as yet no clue to the culprits. We were right, I think in saying they were young men, and one of them almost a lad."

"Yes, quite so," said Mr. Dawes, "the youngster was about the height and build of my friend William here, the other a little older." This directed all eyes on William, who looked sheepish and uncomfortable.

"And you said it was near by the turning up to the mill?"

"Yes, just by there; you know the place, William, I dare say," said Mr. Dawes.

"No, I don't," said William. "Why should I know it?"

"Oh!" said Mr. Dawes, "I thought I had met you just there; but perhaps I am mistaken."

"You never were more mistaken in your life," said William sullenly, and he got up from the table and without further ceremony left the room.

"Whatever are you up to with William?" said Sir Richard, with some amusement. "He can't stand banter. But your questions were innocent enough."

"Well, I can't tell you now," said Dawes. "I hope I shall not have to tell you by-and-by."

Leaving the house the hopeful youth was striding across the wildest part of the common, through woods and bracken to the valley beyond. At the end of a lane that joined the high road leading to the county town five miles away, stood a humble hostelry, where, under the sign of the "Bald-faced Stag," good accommodation was promised for man and beast. It was a solitary house in a lonely part of the road, and bore a dubious reputation for the company it kept.

The bar was full of men, drinking and smoking, and exchanging banter with the bouncing red-cheeked barmaid, who received William as he entered with a smile and a nod of recognition.

Sitting rather alone in a corner, with a jorum of ale before him, was a man, well-dressed in a riding-suit, with top boots and spurs, a lace cravat not over-clean, and a hat drawn rather over his brows so as to obscure his features. With his coarse affectation of fashion, this gentleman, like Gil Blas' acquaintance, Captain Rolando, *ne laissait pas d'avoir l'air d'un franc fripon.*

"Well, my buck," said he, as William made his way through the crowd and sat beside him, "and what brings you here today? Hi! Betsy, a tankard for this gentleman, and fill mine up again."

"Nay, nay," said William, "I dare not stay, I shall be missed and must get back. But hark ye," and he whispered something in his companion's ear.

The other nodded, and going outside the house the two conferred together a few minutes in a low tone.

"I tell you he has found us out," said William.

"Us! You mean you," said the other sharply.

"Why, you're not meaning to go back on me?" said William. "Remember it was I that put you up to this job; and you got most of the swag—"

"And earned it too," said the other. "What could you have done without me? You were in a funk all the while."

"Well, but Jerry, what am I to do? Dawes means to blow on me, and I'm not going to be hanged alone, you may be sure of that."

"Oh, that's the game, is it," said the other, "Why don't you knock him on the head before he peaches?"

"What, murder him?" said William uneasily.

"Your life or his," said Abershaw. "If he peaches, you'll shake hands with the hangman. I know how to take care of myself. So you can do as you please. And now I shall clear off for the scent grows too hot for me here."

He made his way to the stable, and as William started homewards he saw his confederate gallop away towards London.

Left to himself he began to feel very uncomfortable. That Mr. Dawes suspected him he felt sure. Though he had been inspired to deeds of daring by Abershaw, into whose company he had got by frequenting the Bald-faced Stag, and whose reputation as the most notorious highwayman of the day had made him a hero in his ill-regulated mind, William was at heart a coward. He feared detection and its consequences, and would prevent it at all costs.

And then Jerry Abershaw's evil counsel recurred to him. To murder Mr. Dawes before he peached. That was horrible: though he hated the man, he could not go as far as that. And yet, if it would save his neck—why then! But there was hitherto only suspicion, and no proof. He need not decide yet, and would wait till Mr. Dawes made another move. At all events he would be safer away from home, and would make an excuse for going away for a while.

At supper, therefore, he announced his intention of going on a visit to some cousins he had in Essex.

"And when do you start?" asked his aunt. "And how long shall you be away?"

"I go tomorrow," said William, "and I daresay I shall be away some weeks."

"Do you ride there?" asked Sir Richard.

"Yes, uncle—I will ride Daisy, and take my valise with me on her back. There will be some hunting down there and she will carry me well."

Mr. Dawes was looking at William steadily all the while. "Do you ride alone," he asked, "or shall you have a companion with you?"

"No. I have no companion," said William sullenly.

"Why, that's a pity," said Mr. Dawes, "two is better than one on the highway nowadays."

"What do you mean by that?" asked William.

"Oh! Nothing," said Mr. Dawes, while Sir Richard and my lady looked with some surprise from one speaker to the other.

"By the way, Sir Richard," said Mr. Dawes, "I have a clue to the scoundrels who robbed me, and I hope it will lead to their discovery."

"Indeed: that is good news," said his host.

"Yes. I can't tell you just yet, but the day after tomorrow I trust I shall have proof positive of one of the two at all events to lay before you."

William listened with growing terror. The net seemed closing round him. He had a day, however. Mr. Dawes was not going to tell Sir Richard till the day after his departure. Why was he waiting for that?

He had only to wait till the next morning for the explanation. He was in the stable yard seeing to the equipment of his mare, when Mr. Dawes found him, and putting his arm through William's led him, all reluctant, into the garden.

"So you are going into Essex, William," said he.

"Yes," said William, "I am. What is that to you?"

"Why, nothing at all to me," said Mr. Dawes. "But it may be convenient for you. Shall you be near Harwich?"

"Not very far from it," said William.

"Well, William, at Harwich you will find a packet two or three times a week for Antwerp or Rotterdam. Why not take a trip abroad for a few months, or perhaps longer?"

"Why should I?" said William.

"Why should you? Why, because this air does not suit your constitution. It is not wholesome for you."

William was silent for a few minutes. At last in a low voice he said, "What do you say that for?"

"Come, come, William," said Mr. Dawes, "you know that very well. I'm an old friend of your uncle and aunt, and do not wish to see them brought to shame. I shall not tell them what I know till I learn that you are safe out of the way; I'll give you a week's start, but then I must tell them what I know of their nephew. They ought to know whom they are harbouring under their roof. I have connections abroad in Holland who might be able to befriend you and I will write to them on hearing you are landed safely. This will enable you to break with your old associates and reform your life. You will want some money; here are twenty guineas, and these with the ten or twelve I believe you already have of mine will give you a start. So now, farewell; think of what I have said, and resolve to lead a new life."

William, as he rode away, did indeed think of what he had just heard. "After all," he said to himself, "old Dawes had behaved handsomely to him." That he could not deny. But on the other hand he was sending him into exile, perhaps for life. What was twenty guineas to that? And he could not bear that his uncle and aunt, for whom he felt as much affection as lay in his nature, should be acquainted with his real character. And the old home too; was he never to see that again? In spite of the twenty guineas that jingled in his breeches pocket, he felt Mr. Dawes had done him an injury, and his old hatred revived with double force.

His good mare, Daisy, carried him briskly to London. And when he repaired to a hostelry in the Borough with which he had been made acquainted by his evil genius, Abershaw, who, he supposed, would by this time be far away pursuing his trade in a new district. However, on entering the bar parlour the first person he saw was that worthy with a pot of ale before him. William did not want to meet him, and would have shirked away, but the other beckoned to him.

"And what evil wind blows you here," said he. "Why do you follow me?"

"I didn't know you were here," said William. "I am going away for a bit till I can go safely back."

"Has the old man peached?" asked the other.

"No, but he will in a few days' time," said William. "He told me so himself."

"And are you going to let him, you young fool?" said Abershaw. "I'm ashamed of you. Here, come, listen to me," and their further conversation was carried on in whispers. It was evening before William remounted his mare, Daisy, to continue his journey.

About a week later, when the family were at supper in the hall, Mr. Dawes being still with them, a figure approached through the darkness, and entered the house by a back way, with which it was evidently familiar. The servants were all engaged in the kitchen or in attendance in the hall, and no one saw the intruder creep silently up the fine old carved oak staircase to the top storey.

On reaching the room occupied by Mr. Dawes, which looked backward into the garden, he struck a light, and opening a door entered a short dark passage. A narrow winding stair led thence to a turret on the roof of the house, but half-way up, a carefully concealed door admitted him to a small chamber artfully hidden in the hollow of the roof. It had been a hiding place in former days, such as were frequent in old houses during the times of civil commotions, and its existence had almost been forgotten.

An hour or two later Richard Dawes came to bed. He had been anxiously expecting a letter from Holland to report William's arrival, but in vain.

"I suppose the young fool has had sense enough to go. I have given him a week's law. He ought to be safe now," thought he. "So I will tell Sir Richard tomorrow what I know of his hopeful nephew. It will grieve him and my lady sadly, but it may save them future grief by and by, and may prevent that young rascal from continuing his career towards the gallows." With these reflections the worthy Richard Dawes went to bed and was soon snoring comfortably.

The door of the secret passage was silently opened, and a figure cautiously entered. Taking something from the dressing table, the intruder approached the bed. There was a slight struggle, a sickening sound, a gush of something, and then silence. The figure noiselessly crept downstairs the way it had come, and left the house. No one heard the sound of horse's hoofs as he rode away in the dead of the night.

Next morning Sir Richard and Lady Hetherington were roused by shrieks, and servants bursting into their room told the dreadful news. Mr. Dawes had been found in his bed with his throat cut from ear to ear, and the room was deluged with blood. By the bedside was found one of Mr. Dawes's own razors, with which the deed had evidently been done, for it was covered with blood.

The murderer had left no trace. A little later, however, it was observed that the back door was found unfastened. The door leading to the turret stair was ajar, and someone had evidently been in the secret chamber. Later still a groom reported that the gate of the stable yard stood open when he came to his work in the morning, so that the criminal had probably escaped that way.

"A rummy thing too," said the man to himself, "I see the marks of horse's hoofs in the yard and if I didn't know Master William was away with Daisy, I could have sworn it was her footmarks, for her off hind foot is shod peculiar."

"Probably an old mark before she went away," said Sir Richard, when this was pointed out to him. But the old stableman did not seem convinced.

At the inquest a suggestion was made that it was a case of suicide. The razor, it was pointed out, was Mr. Dawes's own. But both sir Richard and Lady Hetherington testified that Mr. Dawes had gone to bed in his usual spirits, after passing the evening agreeably in their company, and that he had no troubles of any kind to worry him. Besides which, there were obvious signs that someone had hidden in the secret chamber and afterwards escaped by the back door. Mr. Dawes was not known to have any enemies, and yet, as nothing had been taken from his room, the motive of the crime did not seem to be robbery. The only verdict the coroner's jury could return was that of "Wilful murder by some person or persons unknown."

It was past midnight on the fatal evening of the murder when William rode into the yard of the hostelry in Southwark where we have seen him before. His mare had been ridden hard, and was covered with foam and sweat as he gave her to the stable-man, but that was no unusual thing in that establishment, and it was the rule there to ask no questions about the going and coming of the customers.

Mounting hurriedly to his bedroom, William threw himself in his clothes, on the bed. He thought with horror of what he had done. "It's all Abershaw's doing," he said to himself. Left alone he would never have brought himself to such a deed. He thought of Mr. Dawes's proposal that he should go abroad for a time and start a new and better life, and he would have given worlds, now it was too late, to have listened to it.

All the events of that horrible night recurred to his memory. He enacted the whole scene again. His ride to the house, his secret entry and climb to the fatal room, and then—oh, God! What had he done? He could not sleep, but got up, paced the room for hours and then sat desolately at the window till the morning light came and showed him some dark stains on his clothes, that made him shrink with horror. With soap and water he tried to wash them out, but in vain. There they were, evidence for his conviction. What was to be done? He changed his dress from his valise: the clothes with the tell-tale stains should be burned, and meanwhile he hid them carefully under the mattress.

And then, what was to be his course now? To return home, to that house on which he had brought the stain of guilt, where he had spent a childhood of innocency, where lived the uncle and aunt who had brought him up and been as parents to him, and which was the scene of that night's atrocity, was abhorrent to him. He felt that he could never go back but must fly the country as he wished he had done when his victim had proposed it. Yes, he would get to Harwich again and hide himself for ever in a strange land.

However, unstable and irresolute as ever, William put off his departure from day to day, and hung about London till his purse was nearly empty, and he found there was not enough left to do more than pay his passage. To land penniless in a foreign country, of which he did not even know the language, seemed impracticable. He began to think that after all he would have to face the return home which he could not contemplate without terror. But some weeks had passed, his feelings were less alive than at first to recollection of the past, and he had almost resolved to write to his uncle and announce his intended return, when, on coming down one morning, he met Abershaw.

His immediate impulse was to avoid him. Abershaw was the cause of all his crimes and all his misery. He would have no more to do with him. But Abershaw was not so easily got rid of, and taking William by the arm, he led him to a quiet corner of the yard, where they were alone.

"Well," said he.

"Let me go," said William. "I'll have no more to do with you."

"Nay," said Abershaw with a sneer; "old friends don't part like that."

"You've brought a curse upon me," said the other. "I wish I had never seen you. I tell you again I have done with you."

"Aye, aye," said Abershaw, "but I've not done with you, my buck. Remember, I know your secret."

"Why, what do you mean? Do you mean to betray me?"

"That depends," said Abershaw, "on whether you do what I tell you or not."

"But who would believe you? You dare not appear, for you are in danger of arrest yourself, and the gallows if you are caught."

"That's well pleaded, Master William," said the other, "and true enough. But what is there to prevent my writing a letter to the magistrates without my name to it? I could tell them certain things about you that would put a halter round your neck. Eh? What do you say to that?"

William could find nothing to say to it, and stood aghast at the prospect before him. He felt himself in the power of this ruffian, and unable to escape.

"Come, come," said Abershaw, "don't be downhearted about what you did. Remember, it was your life or his. By this time he would have given information to your uncle, and you would have been in quod. Now you have made yourself safe like a brave fellow. Come, cheer up. I'll not be hard upon you."

"My uncle would never have prosecuted me," said William, "nor do I now believe Mr. Dawes would. He even offered to befriend me if I went abroad."

"Well, then," said Abershaw lightly, "I daresay they would not. But now you've cut his throat, and I know it, and if I am to hold my peace you'll have to do what I tell you."

"What do you want me to do?" said William sullenly.

"I'll tell you, the," said the other. "I've been unlucky of late, and the locker is empty and must be refilled. The high-roads are watched and there is little to be done there just now. I must crack a crib. Now you say your uncle has a fine lot of silver plate which he could very well spare to me, and you must help me to get it."

"I'll do nothing of the kind," said William indignantly.

"Oh, yes you will," said the scoundrel. "All I want you to do is see that the backdoor is open on the night I tell you, and I will see to the rest."

"I'll not do it. They have always been good to me, and I would not hurt them to save my life."

"Not even to save your life?" asked Jerry, with an ugly leer. "Just think," and with a significant motion of his hand to his neck and his cravat he suggested the fatal noose.

William turned pale. He was, as has been said, at heart a coward. His companion let the idea work, and watched the change in his countenance with attention. At last he said:

"There shall be no harm done to the old people, nor to anybody, nor do I want you to help. All I will have to you do is to see that when the household is asleep the backdoor shall be left open. I and my pals will do the rest. Come, that's little enough. And your uncle is rich, and can afford to let me have a share of his silver plate and be none the worst for it."

"Will you swear not to hurt anyone in the house?" asked William.

"I'll swear by all the gods," said Abershaw; "nobody shall come to harm. I only want the silver."

"And if I do this will you leave me alone in future?" asked William.

"Aye, that I will. I shall have done with you then, and you'll be no further use to me."

The wretched youth felt himself powerless, and in the end promised to do what was demanded of him. It was arranged that William should return home within three or four days, and that the robbery should be made on that day week.

As they parted a figure moved out from a corner close by, and walked slowly away. They only saw its back, the back of a well-dressed gentleman of middle age. Jerry laid his hand on his pistol, and William changed colour.

"Who's that?" whispered Abershaw. But William did not answer. The figure bore a dreadful likeness to one he dared not face.

"'Tis he!" whispered he after a minute or two, while the figure slowly retired up the yard. When it reached the house it turned and looked steadfastly at the pair, who stood spellbound. The face was that of Richard Dawes. In another moment it was gone.

For the rest of the day William had an uneasy feeling that he was watched. That someone was near him following his movements, whom he could not see. He dreaded the night, and feared to be alone. Even Abershaw's company would be better than none, but that worthy had gone off on business of his own leaving William with final instructions, and an assurance that he would be as good as his word if William failed to obey him in the least particular. At night he was haunted by dreams of Richard Dawes, of his terrible crime, and of the gallows. As the days passed he grew pale and thin, and trembled on the least suspicion that anyone looked at him with more than usual attention. He had written home to say he was returning from his visit to Essex, and sir Richard and his aunt were expecting to see him ride in any day.

It was within three days of the time appointed by Abershaw for the robbery that William decided to go home. The feeling that all his movements were watched, and that some unseen presence was ever near him, had never left him, and it inspired him with a growing terror. As the fatal day grew closer this sensation grew stronger, and William constantly felt that at any moment the influence that haunted him might be put on a visible form.

As he mounted his mare Daisy in the evening, when night was already closing in. The sky was lurid and threatening, and thunder was growling in the distance. There had been a sultry feeling in the air all day, and everything portended a storm of unusual violence. Before he had passed the last house of the London suburbs a few large drops of rain began to fall, and the thunder grew louder and more frequent. He cared not; his mind was reduced to such a state of passive misery that external trouble did not affect it; there was even something in the turmoil of the elements congenial to his disordered temperament. The storm burst on him in full fury when he reached the outskirts of the wild common, across which the last few miles of his journey lay.

His horse was fidgety and frightened by the lightning, which now became incessant, and it was then that William first became aware that he was no longer alone. By his side and within a yard of him rode another horseman, keeping exact pace with him as if he had been his shadow. His face was hidden and his movements were silent. But although they were on turf and heather and the footfall was soft, and , moreover, the storm was enough to deaden other sounds, still the noiseless riding of his companion was unnatural.

A dread fell upon him of something unearthly. The figure kept exactly even with him, riding faster or slower as he quickened or slackened his own pace. Each flash of lightning showed him still by his side, silent and mysterious, not to be shaken off. William realised in this ghostly companion the hitherto unseen presence that had haunted him for days. Horror seized him; he dared not take his eyes off from that ghostly figure. A more vivid flash than usual showed him his companion with his face now turned to him, the face he dreaded of all others, and oh, horror" across the throat a gory line.

William shrieked with terror. The horse, frightened to death by the flash and the crash of thunder that followed instantaneously, bolted like a mad thing across the common towards its well-known stable; the stable-yard gates were shut, the horse checked its career, slipped, fell, and threw the rider violently against the wall, where he lay insensible, and as one dead.

The tempest gradually abated, the thunder rolled farther and farther away, morning broke, and the men coming to work found William still insensible lying on the road, and the mare Daisy standing trembling by him. They lifted him up and alarmed the household; he was put to bed in his old room and messengers were sent for the doctor.

After a time William was restored to consciousness, but his mind wandered. He talked as if in his sleep; the watchers by his bedside caught incoherent scraps of sentences. They heard the name of Dawes frequently, with cries of "take him away, take him away." His rambling about Jerry and a backdoor puzzled them. "Keep it locked," he would repeat over and over again, until at last he sank into a troubled sleep.

He had been terribly injured in his fall, and the doctor held out no hope of saving his life. A few days at the longest must end it and his sufferings. As the end approached, his mind became more calm, and he was able to think and talk rationally. He still repeated, however, his warnings to keep the backdoor locked, which they thought was a relic of his former delirium, but he never rested till he was assured that his warning had been attended to.

On the last day, when he knew he was near his end, he asked to see Sir Richard and his aunt alone. They remained with him some time, and when they came out the tears were in their eyes.

"Poor William!" said Lady Hetherington. "What a story! To

think of all this going on while we knew nothing."

"He will die easier, now he has made a confession," said Sir Richard. "I see now what puzzled us in Richard Dawes's behaviour to him. He recognised his voice, and led him to betray himself by his ingenious way of questioning."

"Poor Mr. Dawes!" said she. "He would have been a good friend to William, had not the other man got him into his power and persuaded him to his ruin."

"Yes—the scoundrel! I shall never rest till I hear he has come to the gallows that as sure as death awaits him."

The tragic events of the past few weeks gave sir Richard a distaste for the old house of which he had been so fond, and before long he sold it. Since then it has passed through many hands; it has been occupied and visited by statesmen and heroes of victories by land and sea. Afterwards it was a school for eighty years before once more becoming a private residence. The tradition of a murder was kept alive; boys who slept near the fatal room felt a hot disagreeable shudder when they remembered the legend, and former pupils who often come to see again the scene of their schooldays, invariably ask for "murder chamber," and beg to be allowed to revisit it.

Jerry Abershaw, it may be mentioned in conclusion, was hanged on Kennington common on August 3rd, 1795. He was arrested at the "Three Brewers" in Southwark—the inn he frequented, and he shot one of his captors dead, at the same time accidently wounding the landlord in the head. He died a hardened ruffian at the age of twenty-two.

His mother, foreseeing in his youth the end to which he was bound to come, had prophesied he would, as the saying went, *die in his shoes*. To prove she was mistaken he kicked them off at the last moment. His body was gibbeted on the Portsmouth Road at the foot of Wimbledon Common, the scene of his most famous exploits, and Jerry Abershaw's gibbet lasted long enough to be mentioned in one of Captain's Marryat's novels.